Finding May

By Ian Banks-Jones

Jo, Orla & Finn. Thanks for letting me visit this crazy world I ended up inventing. I am so grateful. Andy, Liam, Nathan & Nev. You guys are something else. Up the F91!

Massive thanks to Scott, Laura & Bronwen for telling me where I was wrong, and Jutiar for seeing just what I had been writing about. Without your photo, I dread to think what the cover would have looked like!

For Susan, Sean & Gelda

Chapter 1

"We are getting reports from the Metropolitan Police that they have confirmed the death of the singer, May Mornington, at the age of twenty-seven. Ms Mornington was reported to have been discovered unconscious at home by her agent earlier today. The London Ambulance Service were in attendance, and they have confirmed that a twenty-seven-year-old woman was pronounced dead at the scene. The cause of death is unknown at this time."

 Jessica would probably have made faces of contrition and felt pangs of sadness had she been aware of the words of the newsreader. She would have reflected on the fact that yet another beautiful and talented woman, this time less than three years younger than her, had had her life cut tragically short by the troubles and pressures of super-stardom. She would have choked with the sadness of losing an old friend, with whom she now hardly spoke. The smoking double-barrel of grief for the person, and guilt for losing contact. She didn't do this, however. She was far too busy, laying asleep, apparently semi-comatose on the living room sofa.

 The light from the television news danced carelessly on the darkness of Jessica's living room walls as she slept. Her fifth floor flat rang with the sound of the television, now far too loud for this time of night.

Jessica's slumber was only interrupted by the shrill ringing of the doorbell. Bleary-eyed, she stumbled clumsily down the length of her hallway to answer, adjusting her messy brown hair and old black leggings as she went. She knew immediately that it would be the pizza delivery driver. Over the last few weeks, he'd become something of a regular visitor. The doorbell impatiently rang again, just as she got there. She could make out his brightly coloured uniform through the frosted glass door before she opened it.

"Hiya love. Medium vegetarian with chicken bites, isn't it?" The driver smiled as he handed over the boxes.

"Yes. Thanks."

"Actually, you know what? I've got a bottle of orangeade going spare if you're interested, darlin'."

"Yes, please. That would be nice." She stepped outside the flat and on to the open, glass fronted landing, as the driver passed over the bottle. "Wait there. I'll be back in a minute." She ran inside with her food. Rummaging through her handbag, she found her purse, and pulled out a shiny two pound coin. She ran back to the front door. "There you go. Have a good evening." She smiled unconvincingly.

"Cheers, love. Enjoy! See you soon." He turned and walked along the landing as she closed the door, perhaps a little too forcefully.

Jess turned the angle-poise reading lamp on and grabbed the remote control as she sat against the arm of the comfy sofa. She curled her legs up underneath her, and flicked the television channels until she found a repeat of a comedy programme. As she put the remote down, she picked up her mobile phone, stared at it briefly, and threw it down next to the pizza. She began eating.

It had taken a number of failed attempts to find a decent pizza place in Jess' corner of South-West London, but this one seemed to be the best that she had found. It wasn't exactly spectacular, but it was reasonably cheap, and the chicken bites were the tastiest she had ever had. She had given up thinking about the calories. It wasn't like she wasn't trying to please or impress anybody right now. She didn't even have to worry about fitting into her work clothes. She dipped the last soft pizza crust into her honey and mustard dip, burped under her breath, excused herself to an otherwise empty flat, and slowly drifted into another deep slumber.

It could have been minutes or hours later when she woke. When she did, it was with a huge start. Suddenly she was completely convinced that she wasn't alone. Within seconds, her worst fears appeared to become harsh reality. As she came to, she became aware of a noise that sounded like the bathroom toilet flushing. Nervously, she grabbed the remote control, switched the television off, and headed cautiously towards the bathroom door, as her heart pounded in her throat.

Chapter 2

A flat with Nick had felt like the most natural thing in the world. The two years leading up to moving in had been a rollercoaster of chaos and romance. Even before they got together, he seemed to go to the same bars as her; he was at every house party she went to, he even knew people who went to her music college. She found herself drawn to his sharp suits, and sharper, stubbly jawline. To start with, he hadn't even tried to look beyond her long, shapely legs, or her wavy brown bob. When they did start to go out together, it seemed so natural, so easy. Jess was finishing her last year studying for a music degree. After a lifetime of dedication to practicing musical instruments, she could feel her enthusiasm for it failing. Endless guitar, piano and musical theory, that had once been as important as the blood in her veins, was now little more than an inconvenience that stood between her and post-graduate life in the real world. She couldn't wait to be free of it all.

Nick managed to make the transition from student life so easy for Jessica. She swiftly found a steady, if unchallenging office job in an advertising agency, and carried on living in her old student house-share. Verity and Matilda were quiet, inoffensive housemates, who usually kept themselves to themselves. Nick would stay over now and then, and occasionally, Jess would stay with Nick. He shared with two irresponsible and untidy guys. Curtis seemed to make his money by means unknown and, as Jess suspected, illegal, whilst Tyler was still a chaotic and immature student at the London School of Musical Performance, the college from which Jessica had just graduated. Unwittingly, it had been Tyler who had brought the two together, introducing them properly at a party in a small downstairs snooker club in Wandsworth.

Things had progressed steadily from there. They had regular dates at their local Nando's, went to the pub to watch gigs, and walked hand in hand through the park together. When Jess had asked Nick about moving in together, he'd been quite happy to agree.

They made the decision to move in to a neatly furnished flat in a block on the edge of Wandsworth. A few homely touches made the flat feel comfortable. On their first week living together, sitting on worn-out, second-hand sofas, Nick had come home with a brand new guitar for Jess, an Epiphone Dot in a blueberry burst. Nick had chosen it 'to match your eyes'. Jessica adored it. She hung it on the living room wall, only playing it occasionally. Jess had returned the favour with the finest suit she could afford for him. He looked thoroughly handsome. The two of them enjoyed their life together, young and carefree. At Jess' insistence, they saved for a deposit on a house, but when they could, they enjoyed nights out in Camden, Hoxton and Soho. When they couldn't, they enjoyed nights in with jazz, blues and wine. Usually, both would be followed with clothes cast to the corners of the bedroom, before ending up asleep in each others arms. Life really was idyllic.

Then, after six years of apparent bliss, a fairytale proposal in Budapest, and consideration of a small dog, Jessica's world came crashing down. It started when Nick got fired from his job working in middle-management for a clothing company. He had claimed that it wasn't his fault, but Nick had apparently tried to cover up one of his colleagues who had been stealing high-end designer jackets. Not long after that, Jess had found a series of suggestive messages and pictures to and from a former workmate called Emma on Nick's phone. Nick assured Jess that it had never gone further than his mobile and begged for forgiveness. For a while, Jess had toyed with the idea of trying to get beyond it, but she soon realised that this was a betrayal too far, and she had to end it immediately. Duly, Nick was sent packing to his parents. Within a few months, Jess had tried her best to forgive him, but she knew that she and Nick would never be anything more than acquaintances on reasonable terms. Even this broke down when she saw Emma and Nick walking around Sainsbury's together one Saturday morning.

Things had fallen further still when, some six weeks short of May Mornington's untimely death, Jess too had found herself without work. The agency that she worked for had undergone 'streamlining'. Jess was offered a generous redundancy package, and she took it without fight. Between her savings and redundancy, Jess had calculated that she could afford three or four months away from work if she needed to, affording her the time to get her head together, and do some re-training.

So, after six weeks, Jess had spent most of her time drinking, eating and watching films. In that time, she had spent more time throwing up than training. Other than her weekly shop, and the twice-weekly alcohol top-up trips, she had left the flat only once; an abortive jog that had seen her home and crying in the bathroom within fifteen minutes. Food deliveries were swiftly becoming her only interaction with the outside world. Jess wasn't overly concerned, though. Even she had been amazed at how quickly she had become accustomed to solitude. Hell, most definitely was other people. How far she had fallen. Jess was rapidly heading towards rock-bottom. The only question was whether she would be conscious when she landed.

Chapter 3

Jess turned silently towards the kitchen. As she had come to, she had realised that a remote control, no matter how big and fancy, would be virtually useless against an intruder. With shaking hands, she rummaged through the cutlery drawer. Eventually, she found a large black-handled chef's knife. It had been a moving in present from Nick's parents, along with the rest of the set, but it had barely had any use in the last few months. Jessica hoped that she wouldn't be using it now either, but she grabbed it all the same. She was completely opposed to violence, but this was no time for morals.

She edged carefully along the wall of the kitchen towards the bathroom door. With each step, she began to feel her heart beat louder and louder through her body. Her legs felt tight, but hollow, as adrenaline coursed through her veins. As she gripped the knife, she could feel her own fingernails digging into her palm. She squeezed as hard as she dared, forcing the blood away from her alabaster knuckles.

Slowly, Jess reached the doorway to the bathroom, left slightly ajar as it often was. She could hear the insistent buzz of the ventilation fan, but only just over the white noise of the sea of blood pounding through her ears. As she stood there, she could feel her cheeks starting to flush as the heat prickled up her neck and across her face. Jessica's entire body was beginning to burn.

"J-just come out now." She shouted hesitantly. "I know you're in there, and I've got a knife. I will use it, you know."

She waited. All the possible scenarios ran through her head, each one less plausible than the last. At first, she thought it might be Nick. Her hazy mind couldn't remember if he had ever handed back his key. Then she remembered the old man, Mr Bailey, next door. He had taken a spare a year or so ago to water their plants whilst they were on holiday. Could it be him? Or perhaps it really was an intruder, making a burglary attempt that had gone wrong. Then again, maybe it was something far worse, somebody there *because* of her rather than despite her. She'd read about attackers who would break in and do horrible things to their victims. If she was lucky, then perhaps it would be quick, and she'd be dead in seconds. If she wasn't…

"Get the fuck out of my bathroom now, whoever you are." She yelled, almost surprising herself with her assertiveness and language in the process.

Jess waited for several minutes, expecting a response at any second. As she stood there, her mind was still racing. Had she even locked the front door? Had somebody forced the lock and got in without her noticing? She took a deep breath and slowly stood in front of the bathroom door. She held the knife aloft. With a sharp kick, Jessica swung the bathroom door open and leapt in, roaring loudly.

Slowly, she spun around. Confusion began to replace fear as Jess realised that she was the only person standing in the bathroom. Her hand, the one holding the knife, fell to her side. She studied the bathroom. Black slate floor tiles and a stylish white bathroom suite hurt her eyes in the stark bright light. The glass shower screen afforded no hiding place either. Just to satisfy her fears completely, she closed the door. All that looked back at her was her fluffy white towelling dressing gown and her green and blue tartan pyjamas, hanging from the hooks.

Jessica's shoulders finally fell as she realised that it had been nothing more than her imagination. Wasting no time, she quickly changed into her pyjamas, brushed her teeth, returned the knife to the kitchen drawer, checked the front door which was still locked, and went to bed. Jess lay in her cold bed, still confined to the left side, on which she always slept. As she switched off her bedside lamp, the pizza, the alcohol, all of her issues and the dissipating adrenaline all seemed to hit at once. Feeling sick in a spinning room, Jessica dissolved into tears. This wasn't the first time that she had cried herself to sleep in the last few weeks.

It was only when she was awoken at just after nine in the morning by a stream of March sunshine pouring through the window, that Jess realised that she hadn't even closed the curtains. The light of the sun and the warmth of the central heating gave the illusion that it was a far nicer day than it actually was. Still, spring was on the march, and gaining momentum daily. She had woken with a sense of positivity. It was as if the traumas of the night before had purged the disappointment from her soul. She felt alive as she stretched and yawned. A small smile began to make its way to her lips.

"Mornin' love. I was wonderin' when you were gonna stir." Standing in the bedroom doorway was a young woman wearing an impossibly short black skirt with a large mohair jumper hanging down over one shoulder. Her dyed black hair was pulled into a loose, low ponytail. Almost comically large sunglasses sat on the bridge of her nose. She was holding a large mug in one hand, and a bottle of bourbon whiskey in the other.

"W-who are you?" Jess stuttered, fear making her insides fold in on themselves.

"It's alright, Jess." The woman held up the mug and bottle, a growing grin on her face. "I've got my breakfast here."

"Just answer my question. Who the fuck are you, what the fuck are you doing here, what the fuck do you want, and how the fuck did you get in?"

"Oooh. Get you. You never used to swear. Ever."

"Well, I never used to get intruders in my flat." Jess pulled up the covers around her neck.

Fear had overtaken her anger. Nerves were etching themselves on Jessica's face.

"I'm not an intruder, am I?" The woman used the mug and bottle to present herself half-heartedly. "It's only me, innit Love."

"I still don't know who you are." Jess was pulling her quilt around her. The woman pulled out a packet of cigarettes from inside her bra. She put one to her lips, and tried to light it, unsuccessfully.

"Have you got an ashtray, Jess?" Jess was so scared, she was on the edge of tears. Her insides were twisting. She wanted this to be over.

"Please, just tell me. Who the FUCK are you?"

"Jess, look." She took off her shades and looked directly at her earnestly. "It's me, Mags."

Chapter 4

"Hurry up, you two. We'll miss the train" Tyler shouted across the traffic of a drizzly, dreary early evening Trafalgar Square. Darkness was starting to steal away the last of the autumn day.

"Who's on fire? Where's the rush?" Nick shouted back, buses and cars almost severing the conversation. Jess clung on to Nick's arm affectionately.

"Come on. I told Mags we'd meet her on the platform. She'll be waiting down there on her own for us. We'll never find her at this time of day." Tyler urged desperately as Nick and Jess made a daring dash between a thousand rushing taxis.

"No. What you actually mean is that you *hope* she'll be waiting for you. She doesn't even know us two." Jess smiled as she playfully picked on Tyler.

"No Jess. What it is, is that we're just his cover."

"Cover?"

"Yeah. We're only here to make it look like he isn't as sad, lonely and screwed up as he really is." Nick insisted, pushing his mate and ruffling his hair.

The three of them headed along The Strand, bouncing from one side of the pavement to the other as they messed about pushing each other, noisily. Together, they looked somewhat incongruous as they walked.

Tyler was tall, slim, and scruffy with strong, attractive features and smooth, pale brown skin. His large afro was slowly being tamed by the weather. His jeans were tight and ripped, and he wore a t-shirt and jumper that didn't quite match. Nick was shorter, with immaculate dress sense. He was wearing a sharp white shirt with jeans, finished off with a navy blue tweed frock coat. His only concession to sharp style was a heavy, dark, Mediterranean stubble that only served to enhance his jawline. Jess hung lovingly onto Nick's arm. A long, mousey brown bob rested on the collar of a fitted emerald green coat that completely covered her frayed denim skirt. Dark brown cowgirl boots sat at the other end of her pipe-cleaner legs. Thick black tights were trying in vain to keep them warm. She had to skip slightly to keep up with the two taller men as they walked.

The overcrowded Northern line platform at Charing Cross underground station was hot and stale and smelt of rush hour. Mags sat oblivious to everything around her on a grey metal perch-seat with her guitar in a black flight case at her side. Mags' ridiculously short skirt gave the impression that her seemingly endless legs were even longer than they were. Scruffy blue Adidas trainers and a vintage black leather jacket finished off her outfit. As she sat there, Mags scrolled idly through her mobile phone. She could hear Tyler and his friends before she could see them. She slid her phone into her bra and stood up to greet them.

"About time you showed up." Mags and Tyler embraced lightly and kissed each other's cheeks. She turned to Nick and Jess, still attached to each other, despite the crowds.

"Come on, we're only a few minutes late…" Mags cut Tyler off.

"So then." She turned to Nick and Jess, still attached. "I'm guessing that these two beautiful creatures must be your mates. Tyler probably hasn't told you much about me, so let me fill you in. I am Margaret

Aisling Geraldine O'Sullivan, but everyone calls me Mags. I'm twenty-two and one day I am going to be famous." Her strong cockney accent seemed slightly out of place with her eloquent confidence.

"Like I was about to say, this is Mags." Tyler explained. "And as you can see, she doesn't suffer from a lack of self-belief."

"Too fucking right I don't." She flashed a devilish smile. "If you want something, just do what you need to do to make it happen. Like this guitar. I worked like fuck in shitty little backstreet boozers to get it. Tonight's showcase gig, I pulled so many strings, and begged so many favours to get even the worst slot of the night. And you don't wanna know how many lecturers I had to shag to get a first."

"Don't listen to her. Mags was a brilliant student, and I reckon she deserved every single mark she got." Tyler defended her modesty.

"Perhaps, but I don't think fucking them did my marks any harm. We all got something out of it." She laughed loudly as the other three looked on, agog.

Mags had only just met Nick and Jess, and already she was holding court. She stared towards Jess, trying not to look as though she was checking her out. Her gaze was only broken by Nick, reaching in to greet her.

"It's nice to actually meet you, Nick. Tyler never shuts up about you." She shook his hand and smiled at him.

"Yeah. He's the same about you with me. I'm just pleased that I can finally put a face to the name." Nick smiled back with recognition, as Mags was already turning away towards Jess again.

"So you must be Jess." Mags looked Jess in the eye, took her by the hands, and kissed both of her cheeks. As Mags slowly moved away, her thumb and index finger caught for a brief second on Jessica's middle finger. "I hear we are both star graduates from LSMP. I've heard your name thrown around quite a bit, and I've even seen some of your old uni work. It's nice to actually meet you though, love."

A distant clunking and banging grew louder and louder until it was accompanied by a rush of cooler air and a jam-packed Northbound train.

"Come on. I'm not watching another train go without me. We need to get to Camden. I need to get there. Preferably today. Come on, you lot." Mags shouted as she grabbed her guitar and squeezed herself on board.

Chapter 5

"Fuck off. I don't believe you." Jess shouted, anger quickly overtaking her confusion.

"Look Jess. Just look at me." May Shouted, only half joking. "In fact, wait there."

May marched out of the bedroom door and into the living room. Jess got up, hurriedly and angrily made her bed, and followed behind her.

"I don't know who you really are, or what you are up to. I just want you to get out now. And can you please stop trashing my flat. Look. What is it that you are *actually* looking for?" Jess shouted impatiently.

May rifled through a large neat stack of vinyl albums next to a vintage record player, throwing classic albums across the room, one by one. As she did so, Jess was trying in vain to pick them up, scrambling around on her hands and knees. May was mumbling to herself as she flung them.

"Beach Boys, Boney M, Boney M? Really? Miles Davis, Paloma Faith, Fleetwood Mac, Lady Gaga, The Kinks…" She paused. "Right. Here it is."

"Here what is?" Jess shouted back, exhausting what little patience she had left.

"Ta-da!" May held up a signed copy of an album to her face. It was fronted with a near life-sized photograph of the artist. May Mornington.

"May? Mags?" Jess asked, the wind taken from her sails.

"Finally. She gets it."

"It's been three and a half, no, four…" Jess looked confused, but started to relax slightly. "But what are you doing here? How the fuck did you get in?"

"It's actually been almost four and a half years, love. I stood at the end of your landing for ages, just waiting for you to go out or come back. Then I walked down. I was gonna' knock, and then I saw the pizza guy. I just walked in. Smiled and winked. He didn't give a shit."

"Okay. The odd party, the occasional message or card, free tickets on your tours, and then you just turn up completely out of the blue? You're not answering my question, Mags. What are you doing here?" Jess couldn't decide if she was angry, or pleased to see her.

"Well, after yesterday, I needed somewhere to lie low for a bit. I know, I have been a shit mate, haven't I? I should have been in touch more, I s'pose. But right now, I just need a friendly face." Mags took off her shades, her eyes glassy with tears.

"What happened yesterday?"

"Don't you get the news on the fifth floor?"

"What do you mean?" Jess asked, innocently.

"Just Google me." Mags responded bluntly.

"What have you done this time? Another sex scandal? Fallen out of a nightclub at 4am? Or have you punched a record producer?" Jess rolled her eyes, expecting the usual salacious tabloid headlines. She grabbed her phone and started scrolling.

"Not quite."

Mags stood in front of Jessica with her head bowed, and her arms behind her back like a naughty schoolgirl. Jess scoured the internet, trying to find out what had happened.

"I don't…" Jess looked up. "I don't quite understand. All of this seems to be saying that you're…"

"Yes?"

"It says that you're dead."

"I know." Mags replied, sheepishly. "I think I might need to explain it to you." She finally managed to light her cigarette, and opened the window. "Now, can I have an ashtray please? I've got a bit of a story to tell."

Chapter 6

"Look Tyler, I couldn't give a shit if Camden Town is closer to the pub. We're getting off at Mornington Crescent." Mags growled from her seat on the rush-hour busy tube carriage.

"Come on, Mags. You're being difficult for the sake of it." Tyler responded, apparently exasperated by her awkwardness.

"Ty, just leave it." Jess warned sternly. "People have all sorts of justifications for things. Just because you don't know what they are doesn't make them any less valid. Very little ever really happens for no reason. If Mags wants to get off at Mornington Crescent, then we should respect that."

"Thanks love." Mags readjusted her seat position as she responded quietly. "You didn't need to do that."

"It's not a problem. I get it."

As the train slid to an undramatic halt, Jess, Nick, Tyler, Mags and the guitar case disembarked onto the virtually deserted platform of Mornington Crescent tube station. Compared to Camden, it was quiet, neat and clean. Rich blue and cream tiles adorned the walls and appeared to hark back to its Edwardian origins. The four travellers barely noticed this as they rushed by, nearly beginning to run late for Mags' gig.

"Lift?" Nick enquired as he reached out for the call button.

"Nah. I'm good with the stairs." Mags tried to sound nonchalant.

"You're not afraid of lifts, are you?" Tyler tried to tease, the corners of his mouth creeping up towards a smile.

"No. I. I've got nothing against lifts. I'm not scared. No." Her response came in instalments. She made her point slightly too strongly.

The four of them began to trudge wearily up the staircase, Mags trying to hurry the troops on from the rear. Nick had offered to carry Mags' guitar, before realising that sixty-six steps with a heavy flight case would hardly be a walk in Regent's Park.

"Are you okay with that guitar, sweetheart?" Jessica asked quietly, watching as he began to struggle.

"Don't worry, Jess. He'll be okay. Just look at those big arms and broad shoulders. He's more or less designed for it." Mags laughed, her breath escaping carelessly as she did.

"I'm fine." Nick panted. "There can't be many left now, can there?"

"Not many to go. We're nearly there."

Realisation was hitting Tyler. Mags' words had been playing on loop in his head. Eventually, the penny fell earthwards before landing abruptly at his feet.

"Mags is scared of lifts. Big bad Mags is scared by lifts. I bet that's why you wouldn't get off at Camden Town." Tyler grinned inanely, proud of his moment of insight. Mags did her best to cut him off with an icy glance.

"Tyler. Leave it." Jess urged, sensing Mags' reluctance to reply.

"No, it's alright. I can see he's itching for the truth. It's only fair he gets it." Mags brushed Jessica's arm with her hand, and took a deep, quivering breath. "Camden Town station. Eight years ago, one Friday, straight after school. Me and my mate Julia are going for a nosey around some of the stalls on the market. We're off to meet her boyfriend, Simon. We get in the lift, and I see him. He's been eyein' both of us up since King's Cross. Businessman. Early fifties. Paper under his arm. Respectable looking. Anyway, he stands behind us, right behind me. I know he's there. I can feel the hairs on my neck moving when he breathes out. Then, I feel this hand lifting my little school skirt, running up between the back of my legs. I mean, I'm not a total innocent, not totally naïve, but here we are. I'm in a lift, and this dirty fucking nonce has got his palm on my arse cheek, and his fingers are getting close to my…" Mags paused. "… I'm fucking fourteen, and this wanker thinks that he can just grab my arse, and slip his fingers in my snatch because he's a bloke, and I'm a little girl in a lift who won't dare tell him to stop."

"Fuck, I'm sorry, Mags. I didn't know." Tyler fell silent, shame burning his face.

"Well, I don't exactly put it on my CV."

"I suppose it's understandable that you avoid the lifts at Camden then." Nick offered, more than anything else, to break the shocked awkward silence.

"No. That's not why I avoid Camden Station. That's why I hate lifts."

"So why do you avoid Camden then?" Jess asked, a little confused.

"I got barred from the station for breaking his fucking wrist." Mags replied, without the slightest flicker of irony.

"What?" Tyler was perplexed.

"I turned around, grabbed his hand, and twisted his arm until it snapped. Proper messy break too. See, you can prove a broken wrist, but nobody believes a gobby fourteen-year-old. He more or less got away with it, too. Dirty old bastard."

"You poor thing." Jess responded, almost killing off the ailing conversation completely.

"Still, there was a bright side." Mags said passively, after what seemed like too long of an age. "I bet he was reminded of me every time he fancied a wank. Fuck it, I hope he still does, the filthy paedo."

Mags cackled like a maniac, as they stepped into the street, and began to run towards the Dublin Castle.

Chapter 7

The black plastic kettle clicked as it reached boiling point. Jessica's hands, still shaking visibly, clumsily threw a tea bag into a clean cream mug. She followed it with two teaspoonfuls of sugar, and a cursory splash of skimmed milk.

"Are you sure you don't want a cup, Mags?" Jess shouted over her shoulder from the kitchen.

"I'm still all good here, love." Mags replied loudly from the living room, lifting her half-empty bourbon bottle towards the voice.

Jess walked carefully from the kitchen into the living room, holding her mug. Slowly and deliberately, she sat down on the sofa opposite Mags. Jess had automatically ushered Mags towards a seat near the window. A tickling draught from the open window attempted to blow away the remaining smell of imported Marlboro red cigarettes, but failed to keep pace with the growing blue cloud. Jess was unaccustomed to the smell, and coughed, as quietly and unobtrusively as she could manage.

"Sorry love. I forget sometimes. I'll stop if you want." Mags' hand hovered above a small glass of water that she had poured herself as a makeshift ashtray.

"No. You carry on. I don't really mind." Jess lied. Badly. Mags chose to believe her.

"Cheers."

The pair sat in silence, Mags' eyes scanning the more or less neat and tidy living room. They rested on the album covers that adorned the walls; the wall mounted television and the guitar. Mags was purposely avoiding any eye contact, doing everything and anything she could to hide from the inevitable car-crash conversation that lay ahead. Eventually, Jess found the courage to speak.

"So." She began. "Every news outlet in the western world appears to be reporting your death, yet somehow, here you are in my dodgy little flat in Wandsworth, despite the fact that we've hardly spoken in nearly two years."

"Yeah. I guess." Mags smiled, embarrassed and apologetically. "Surprise!"

"Never mind the fact that I was having my own meltdown before you even showed your face, the way that everything in my world is breaking into absolute smithereens right now, or the fact that I could really do with somebody, anybody to talk to at the moment, and I have absolutely no-one. Not one single person who I can trust. Not one single opinion to help me."

"Well, that's it then. We can be each others' therapy."

"Jesus, Mags. Everybody thinks you're dead. What could you possibly contribute to the world of balanced reason and thoughtful dialogue?" Jess laughed nervously.

"I get where you're coming from, but it's a bit late now, innit?" Mags tried to placate Jess, with little success.

"But do you understand? Really? Can you even tell me what you're doing here?"

Mags paused for what felt like an age, looking for the right way to phrase her answer. She took a slow, deep breath.

"You know what? You'd be surprised just how easy it is to fake a death. All it takes is a half-decent plan, a healthy anonymous trust fund, a couple of generous pay-offs to the right people, and a little leak to the news channels?"

"I beg your pardon?" Jess didn't know whether she ought to be impressed or shocked. She stood up, leaving her cup on the table.

"My agent Annie, two other people and you. That's it. No-one else knows about this." Mags took a mouthful of whiskey. She grimaced as she swallowed. "The hardest part is sorting out plans for the future."

"Who'd have guessed that? It's harder to sort out the future when you're dead." Jess looked at Mags sternly.

Mags' face fell through nervous embarrassment, to laughter, and then into big round tears. Jess instinctively leaned over the back of the chair and put her arms around her.

"Everything is just fucked at the moment. I just wanted everything to stop, or carry on without me. I was feeling like I was public property. I really couldn't take the shit anymore. I had to do something to escape." Mags sobbed.

"I'm really sorry Mags. I'm barely managing to sort my own problems out. I don't know how I can help you."

"Look Jess, I'm not really after anything but a bed for a few nights. I don't think anyone can help me right now, anyway."

Mags dissolved into a mess of tears. Jess squeezed Mags and kissed her hair.

"Whatever it is, we can sort this. I really don't know how, but we can come out of this better. I promise you."

Mags lifted Jessica's hands over her head. She leant forward and put her bottle on to the coffee table. She stood up, straightened her skirt, and used her index fingers to clear the mascara that had run underneath her eyes, and turned to face Jessica, holding her arms out in front of her.

The two women tentatively stepped towards each other and held tightly, both wanting to believe that they were doing it to help the other, but both knowing that they were simply soothing themselves.

Chapter 8

Parkway bends gently away from the centre of Camden and heads up a slight hill towards the Dublin Castle pub. The hustle and bustle of extreme retail, tourist honeypots, shouting pubs and eateries quickly give way to local barbers, neat little delicatessens and estate agents. The Dublin Castle sits amongst these gentrified old buildings, looking like an incongruous lump of faded red and white stucco covered Victoriana.

The Irish navvies who built the Victorian railways to the suburbs and beyond quickly found themselves needing a watering hole. The Dublin Castle was built purely to sate their thirst. Once the railways were completed, many of the Irish dispersed, but the clientele gently shifted over the years. Time has taken it from those navvies and builders, through locals and workers, and on to musicians, hipsters and even the odd lost tourist.

In the late 1970s, it accidentally became the centre of a musical explosion, when a fledgling Madness became the house band. Spooling forward just over ten busy years, Blur were to become the new darlings of North London when they made their bow in the capital there.

Once again, a few years later, it found a niche in musical folklore when it became one of Amy Winehouse's popular haunts. She could regularly be found drinking, playing or even working the bar.

On this particular evening, the street outside reverberated to the echoes of music and talking. A fine drizzle hung in the air, stained orange by the sodium streetlights. The rain did little to dampen the spirits of the drinkers, some spilling out onto the pavement, clutching small khaki boxes of cigarettes, hurriedly lighting, smoking, and extinguishing one before returning inside to warmth and more alcohol.

Mags, Tyler, Jess and Nick were marching towards the Castle with as much speed as the narrow pavements would allow.

"If we're fucking late…" Mags hissed tersely.

"We'll be there in no time. I can see it." Tyler responded, trying to calm her.

"If you'd turned up when you said you were going to, we'd be there now. If Jake has kicked me off the running order, I'm going to proper fuck you up, you just wait." Mags was getting angrier as she walked.

"I'm sorry, Mags. Really, I am. There, are you happy now?"

"No. No, I'm fucking not."

The four of them tried to squeeze through the door at the same time, with predictable results. The interior looked pretty much the same as it probably had for over fifty years. Wooden floorboards, cast iron tables, velour upholstered stools. It seemed that the gentrification of Camden had passed the Dublin Castle by. The place was better for it, too. It felt real, genuine, and had a character that no refurbishment would ever be able to replicate. In the far right-hand corner was a nondescript door that led to the back room. Tonight, it was manned by a surly-looking doorman, looking thoroughly disinterested.

"Sorry guys. It's full in here tonight." He said, not really bothering to look at them.

"It's alright, darling." Mags smiled. "They're with me. I'm playing tonight."

"Course you are, sweetheart."

"No, really. She is." Nick leant forward and pointed the guitar at the doorman.

"You're not on my list. Goodbye." The surly doorman went back to staring in the middle distance.

"You didn't even look." Jess protested.

"Look Miss, the only artists who haven't shown were supposed to be here for their soundcheck nearly an hour ago. Unless you're a band called May Something, then I suggest you piss off."

Mags stepped forward, dusting herself down as she did.

"That's me. I'm May."

"Sorry. I think that Jake had given up on you. There's no surname here. I thought you were a band. I was told that this was a band showcase. Somebody must have given me dodgy information." The demeanour of the doorman changed in an instant.

"Well, there you are. You live and learn. Are we good to go in then?" Tyler went to lead the four in.

"Just you May, I'm afraid, sweetheart. We really are full in here."

"You can't let a girl go in there on her own though, can you? Just me? Unaccompanied?" Mags looked up at the doorman with big, innocent eyes.

"Go on then. Just one more of you though."

Mags reached between Tyler and Nick, grabbed Jess firmly by the arm, and pulled her in front of them. She gave them both an apologetic look, mouthing 'sorry' as she did so.

"What's happening?" Jessica looked slightly terrified and totally confused.

"You're coming with me, love. You don't mind me picking Jess, do you boys?" She turned back to the doorman without waiting for their response. "Thanks, hun. Are we good now?"

"Yeah. In you go. Sorry, what surname shall I put down?"

Mags turned back to Tyler with a wicked glint in her eye. "Mornington. Put me down as May Mornington."

Chapter 9

May picked up her phone from the bedside table. She scrolled to her messages, and began to type.

"Annie, there's a leather bag with a few quid in the living room. Take it and delete this text. You've been the best agent and manager, but I can't take you with me for the next part of my journey. I'm really sorry, but I'm doing it. Just like I said. You know what to do. Who to call. Love ya babes. MMxx"

May found her finger hovering over the send button. A nondescript Monday was in progress, as she slowly drank herself towards oblivion. This morning had seen her working her way through a bottle of Southern Comfort. She found it to be the most palatable of spirits in the morning.

May wasn't far short from genius, with perfect pitch, eclectic taste and a talent for lyrics that managed to speak deeply to everyone that heard them. Her voice was deep and soulful with a gentle rasp, and was equally at home with slow jazz standards or raucous bluesy rock covers. She was like a musical magpie, taking tunes wherever she found them and moulding them to her own unique style. She'd been singing all of her life, and never really felt happy unless she was performing. This wasn't without complications. Even before fame had arrived, she wasn't afraid to party. May would be out as much as she could, drinking, dancing and doing whatever she liked to excess. Often, she would return home with company, and would feel virtually no shame for her actions the following day.

May never sought excuses for her behaviour, but nearly all of her crazy outlandish actions had ready explanations. Not that many people knew them.

Margaret O'Sullivan hadn't had the best start in life. It had only been when her older sister, Bernadette, had died of a drugs overdose, that she found out that Bernie had actually been her mother. Her grandmother, who had brought her up as her own, had herself run away to London from Dundalk in the late 70s whilst pregnant at fifteen. When the same thing had happened to her daughter, she had been determined to make sure that history didn't completely repeat itself, and did what she felt she had to to keep the family together.

Life growing up in a tiny flat with two powerful women in Hackney had been almost unbearably tough, but Mags had always found a way through. She had worked hard at school and managed to pursue her dream of going to music college. She'd never sought fame, and when it did find her, it left her with even less control than she had before.

Just before she started college, Mags' grandmother had died suddenly and unexpectedly of a brain haemorrhage. At just eighteen, she was completely alone in the world. Once again, her sheer hard work and unbelievable ability pulled her through, as she pulled together scholarships, bursaries and bar work and busked a living on tube station platforms.

One day, whilst performing at South Kensington tube station, a small, round, fifty-something man in an ill-fitting suit stopped her, and insisted that she should perform with him. Taking a ridiculous risk, she agreed to meet him in a deserted back street pub in Bermondsey, and so began her musical relationship with Mickey George, the most incongruous, yet talented pianist imaginable.

A year had passed since his untimely demise from prostate cancer, and May struggled to move on without him. He had been there for all of her career, whether it was the back room of a local boozer, or Wembley Arena in front of 15000, 'steady hands' Mickey had been precisely the calming influence that May had always needed.

Five success filled years, and millions of record sales had brought recognition, both good and bad. May's face adorned magazines and newspapers. But, as time went on, the pressures of the music business took her from the culture section of the broadsheets to the front pages of the tabloids. The red tops had yet more quarry.

Not that her record company were all that bothered. Every time she appeared, falling out of a nightclub with a random stranger, another radio station would play her songs and another flurry of YouTube views or album streams would appear. Everyone's a winner, provided the royalty cheque stays healthy.

May was trying to get it together for another album, but self-doubt was eating her from the inside. Creeping remorse for her actions, paranoia and loneliness were taking ever greater slices of her away. The pain of simply carrying on, the weight of expectation, it was rapidly becoming too much.

She became obsessed with the idea of leaving May Mornington behind, and just disappearing off somewhere, away from press scrutiny and prying eyes. Of course, she knew that it was almost impossible to do. Annie, her agent and manager, tried to help her, but trying to get May to change her mind was like trying to get a ship to change course by wafting your hands.

So, this nondescript Monday, this meaningless, grey day was to be her turning point. May sat on the edge of her bed, as she took a large drag on a duty-free Marlboro and lined up two dozen prescription sleeping pills. She ground down her cigarette stub in the stainless steel ashtray as the last wisps of hot smoke burned her nicotine-stained fingers. Margaret finally pressed send, deleted the message, took another swig of Southern Comfort, and locked her bedroom door.

Chapter 10

The back room at The Dublin Castle was jam-packed with people. The mix was noticeably eclectic. A large bunch of young lads in black heavy metal t-shirts and jeans had congregated by the stage, waiting for their mate's band, who were headlining. Elsewhere, small groups of friends gathered in clusters, clutching their drinks as they spoke and laughed. Dotted around the room were several single men with sensible haircuts, mostly in their thirties. Each one was nursing a bottle of beer and looked completely out of place, especially compared to the metal-heads.

"They're the A&R men." May shouted into Jessica's ear as they fought through the crowd.

"Who are?" Jess replied, totally oblivious to them.

"Those geezers." She pointed at one with a notepad, check shirt, and sensible haircut. "The one who looks like someone's dad waiting outside a youth club."

As she spoke, a small middle-aged man in his 50s came barrelling over. His shirt, burgundy with a chunky collar and gold cufflink filled cuffs, gaped between each button, and sat taut on his pot belly. His balding grey hair sat precariously on top of his round face. Gold wire-framed glasses didn't obscure the twinkle in his baby blue eyes.

"Allo darlin'!" He exclaimed, thrusting out his pudgy hands, fingers adorned in sovereign rings.

"Mickey! Alright sweetheart?" May threw her arms around him. "Sorry, Jess. This is Mickey George. He's the best pianist in London. This is Jess, Mickey. She's my new best friend."

"Pleasure to meet you, love." He shook her hand and turned back to May. "Come on Mags, we need to get a wriggle on."

"Yeah, yeah. I know. That wanker doorman wouldn't let me in."

"That's fine love, but we're on first. We ain't even got time for a soundcheck now, Mags." Mickey spoke firmly, but looked gently at May.

"Alright. I get it." She turned to Jess. "Sorry darlin', I'll be back as soon as poss'."

"Don't worry. I came to see you play, I was expecting it."

Mags leant in and kissed Jess on the lips.

"What was that for?" Jess asked, looking confused.

"Just a kiss for luck." She smiled, winking as she did. "Back in a bit."

Jess went to the bar to grab a drink. She had barely had a chance to return to her clearing in the crowd before May had begun to play. Mickey and May seemed to have a natural affinity with each other. As May stood on the stage and sang, the noise of the audience fell to a natural hush. She looked ten feet tall on the stage, confident yet vulnerable. The entire room was watching her, hanging on her every word. She was obviously loving every second of it. May was in her natural environment, the audience mesmerised, following every word and movement.

Jess watched on. Her initial jealousy at May's apparent ease on stage was soon forced aside by her charisma. It wasn't the beauty of her voice, or even the way she moved on the stage. It was something indescribable, beyond conventional explanation.

"So, did you like?" May ran towards Jess as soon as she finished.

"Like it? It was fantastic. You were absolutely amazing." The two embraced like old friends.

"Let's just hope one of these old dudes wants to get into my knickers bad enough to sign me up. What do you reckon, Mickey?" He was wandering over, sweat patches under each arm.

"You were pretty fuckin' good darlin'. You don't need me to tell you that."

"Or me, for that matter. You were, as always, truly amazing Mags." Jake, the event promoter, had joined them without being noticed.

Mags turned around, somewhat taken aback by Jake's unannounced appearance. Quickly, she regained her composure.

"Did you expect anything less from me?" She smiled and kissed his cheek, effortlessly easing her arm around his shoulders.

Jake Elliot had been the lead singer of a minor indie band at the back end of the britpop explosion. Despite positive press, neat melodies and a very nice sound, they had probably arrived on the scene about a year too late. This had robbed Jake of his place amongst britpop royalty, but he had found himself a niche as a promoter of new music in whichever North London venues he could find. He didn't make much, but it kept him busy. His smouldering model looks and dark brown slicked-back hair, once considered to be the most distinguishing feature of his band, had mellowed into rugged handsomeness with salt and pepper temples. Here was a man who had been at every party for almost twenty-five years, drinking little more than lime and soda at most of them.

"Have you met Jake, Jess?" Mickey popped up, a glass of whiskey in his hand.

"Jake? No." He smiled warmly at her. Jessica's eyes remained on him. "I haven't had the pleasure."

"This is Jake. He's just some has-been from some god-awful indie band from when we were little. Apparently, he still thinks he's Billy Big-Bollocks, and puts on these nights to prove it. I think he's having a mid-life crisis. " Mags smiled at him. "And he has some seriously shit handwriting too. Who the fuck is May Something? Was that supposed to be me?"

"What?" Jake looked confused.

"Apparently, I've got a new stage name, thanks to you and your illegible scribble."

"May Mornington? I thought you had re-invented yourself. I, erm, I like it, actually." Jake smiled, sheepishly.

"Because of you, I had to reinvent myself just to get into this shit-hole."

"Well, whatever you do, don't re-invent yourself again just yet, Miss Mornington. There's a guy over here called Paul who wants to have a brief word with you. I have a sneaking suspicion that he might be from a record label. I didn't recognise him, but he seemed suitably impressed with your set."

"Cool. He'd better be quick. Me and Jess are off to a party in Archway in a bit."

"Are we?" Jess was hearing this information for the first time.

"Wish me luck guys. I need to turn on the charm." May reapplied her lipstick, pushed her breasts up and together, and walked over towards Paul, hanging off Jake's arm, hoping to score herself a record deal.

Chapter 11

Jessica stood in front of the cooker in the kitchen of her flat. It was an open plan flat, but the position of the hob left her facing away from the living room where Mags sat. Jess was frying eggs. She watched, almost meditatively, as the edges of the whites slowly turned lacy and golden brown. Carefully, she picked them up one by one, letting the oil drip back into the pan before placing them on slices of soft, white buttered bread. She squirted an oversized dollop of tomato ketchup onto one of them, topped them both with another slice of bread, and carried them through to the living room. She passed the sandwich with ketchup over to Mags.

"So, how long are you planning on hanging around for then?" Jess asked, with no tact whatsoever.

"I just need to wait for the fuss to die down a bit." Mags stuck her nose into a magazine, speaking between mouthfuls of ravenously devoured sandwich. "It'll be fine."

"Don't think I'm trying to get rid of you, I'm really not. You know you can stay for as long as you need to. I'm not going to judge you. I really don't think that's my place."

"I know darlin'. I'm so grateful for this. As soon as I figure out how, I'll see you right too. I promise." Mags seemed distracted. "I'm bustin' for a slash, I'll be back in a min." Mags cast the magazine onto the coffee table, then did the same with her half-eaten sandwich.

Jessica grabbed the magazine that Mags had thrown onto the coffee table and began reading. After a few moments, she noticed that Mags was stood in the doorway, watching her. It was only as Jess looked up that she realised that Mags was stretching apart her thumbs in the waistband of a well-worn pair of Jessica's oversized knickers.

"Fuckin' hell, Jess. It's no wonder Nick the prick fucked off, is it? Look at these bad boys."

"If you had actually spoken to me properly in the last few months, then you would know that it was actually me that told him to go, not the other way around. Things weren't good between us, and I felt like I couldn't trust him anymore." Jess spat back indignantly.

"I didn't even know you could buy pants like this anymore. Do you have to order them online?"

"Can we leave it please Mags? We don't all wear dental floss underwear."

"I'll have you know that my underwear is sensible, but sexy. I haven't even owned a thong in years."

"My underwear doesn't define me. Nick and me didn't split up because of a pair of manky grey knickers."

"Look, I'm just saying what I saw. I didn't want to rock the boat." Mags defended her position.

"Sorry Mags, it still just feels a bit raw." Jess dabbed at the corners of her eyes. "It all got a bit messy towards the end, that's all."

An awkward silence filled Jessica's flat. The two of them sat there, busying themselves with whatever they could. Finally, Mags cracked.

"I stand by calling him a prick, though. Fucking you about makes him a proper bell-end in my book." They returned to silence.

Mags stood up and padded around the flat, examining the ornaments dotted about. She stopped at the beautiful blue guitar, hanging on the wall.

"Do you still play that thing?" She gestured towards the guitar, now slightly dusty.

"Oh God, no. Well, not that often."

"You should. You were ace." Mags smiled, pleased that she had successfully changed the subject.

"I don't… I mean, I hardly ever play these days."

"Just pick it up, love. I'll sing along with you, come on. Please?" Mags looked at Jess, smiling hopefully.

"Really? I haven't played in weeks. I'm not sure I'll be as good as you think. Those recordings were years ago." Jess looked uneasy as she took her guitar off the wall and dusted it down.

"Well, I've been dead for 24 hours, and I'm still going to sing along with you. I don't reckon things get much more fucked up than that. Now stop being such a wuss and plug in that fucking Epiphone."

Chapter 12

The black taxi snaked through the streets of Holloway. May and Jess sat in the back, giggling like two schoolgirls as they headed off to their party.

"Alright ladies. Are you havin' a good evenin' then?" The cabby asked, in a broad cockney accent.

"Well, I've just scored a record deal, and me and my new best friend here are off to celebrate. A mate of mine is having a house party. I don't know about Jess, but I'll be doing my best to get off my tits, and throw up in the pot of a houseplant. It's gonna be ace." Mags blurted out breathlessly.

"Good on you, sweetheart. So, erm, when are you gonna be on Top of the Pops then?" The taxi driver chuckled to himself, apparently amused by the idea.

As he laughed, his head pushed back on the perspex divider. A small roll of fat formed at the back of his head as he did. The cabby wore an ill fitting sleeveless fleece. His laughter lines and thinning, greying hair suggested that he was in his mid-fifties. Every now and then, his hand thoughtlessly dived into a large bag of crisps.

"No. Really. I've just played a showcase gig at The Dublin Castle. I sign with Impact Records on Monday and start recording in a month or two. I couldn't give two shits if you want to believe me or not, that's up to you." All of a sudden, May began to prickle.

"Sorry love, you get a lot of wannabe's around here. I didn't..."

"I'm not a wannabe. I'm the real deal." May stopped abruptly, purposely letting the words hang awkwardly.

Jess could feel herself cringing. The taxi driver began to panic, not knowing what to say for the best.

"Look darlin', I wasn't saying..."

"I know what you were saying. You'll be telling your fares about me in years to come." May started to ease back from anger towards cheeky sarcasm.

"Go on then, what name do I need to remember?" He grabbed himself a small handful of crisps.

"May Mornington. I'll sign one of your receipts if you halve the fare."

"I don't know about that." The cabbie shook his head to himself and smiled, relieved that he had successfully sidestepped the argument. "It's up here, just off the Holloway Road innit?"

"Yeah. Number 26. You'll probably hear it before we get there."

Jess and May giggled to each other, pointing and looking at random people walking by the supermarkets and chicken shops . She may have only known her for a matter of hours, but Jess felt instantly comfortable with May. May's excitement seemed to fill the taxi as they pulled up to the party.

"That'll be £8.40 please, love."

"How about you take my autograph, and we call it a fiver?"

"I don't know darlin'..."

"I'll give you a goodnight kiss as well then."

"I'm a married man, love."

"Well, best not tell your wife about it."

"Alright then, just this once. You'd better become a proper superstar though." The cabbie threw a notebook through the hole in the dividing screen. "Can you write it to Gary?"

May dutifully scrawled a message and her name with a chewed, half-broken ball pen. She handed it back with a crisp five-pound note. A small smile grew as she passed it through the slot. She opened the door, and pushed it wider with her foot, until it swung fully open.

"Thanks. Have a good night." May and Jess skipped away from the black taxi, arm in arm.

"You forgetting something, love?" The cabbie shouted from his open window.

May ran back to the taxi and kissed him passionately. As quickly as she had left, she returned and hooked arms with Jess again.

"Good God, May." Jess smiled. "You really have got some balls. I couldn't do that in a million years."

"It's only a bit of fun. I quite like cheese and onion." The pair laughed. "You should see what I wrote on his notepad."

"What did you put?"

May cleared her throat, shook her head and began.

"To Gary, thank you for giving me the best ride I've had in ages. You really got me there too, much quicker than most guys. Thanks for letting me pay you in kind, Miss May Mornington." May threw her head back as she laughed.

"Whose party is this, anyway?"

"I used to see a guy who lived in Highgate New Town, in one of those weird-looking apartments. Greg. Nice bloke, proper bohemian sort. Everything was great until he went back to his wife. Apparently, I wasn't the 'settling down type'. Fuck him, his loss." May adjusted her hair. "Anyway, this is his son's house-warming party."

"And he invited you? If you were seeing his dad, just how old is he?" Jess couldn't comprehend what she was hearing.

"Noah didn't exactly invite me, but he did have a massive crush on me. He's 19. It's cool. Just follow my lead."

Jess and May walked up the steps of a large three storey shared house. It seemed to be bathed in darkness.

"I thought you said this was going to be a massive party."

"Yeah. Maybe it's just not got going yet." Mags replied, with uncertainty.

"Really?"

"Noah's parties are crazy. Trust me."

May went to knock on the door. As she did, it fell open. Tentatively, they stepped in. Groups of party-goers huddled in small clumps in the hall and dining room. There was no pumping music, no wild atmosphere. Instead, chatter could be heard, along with light jazz. Undeterred, May headed on to the kitchen. She was pleased to see more people. Some were even dancing, but most were congregating around the large quantities of alcohol, sitting on the worktop. May forced her way through the crowds, before she found Noah and tried to hug him. At first, Noah looked confused. After a second or two, he started shouting at May.

"Get out of my house. You're not wanted round here. You screwed up my family once, you're not doing it again."

"Fine. I'm going. You used to be cool. Even when you used to spy around the bedroom door to try to see me in my knickers."

Even in the half-light of the kitchen, it was obvious that Noah was blushing.

"Please, Mags, don't cause a scene. Mum and Dad are in the lounge. Can you just leave without a fuss?"

May looked across to the worktop, and spotted an unopened bottle of vodka, and a 4-pack of beer on the side. She faced Noah and passed the beer to Jess. Without breaking eye contact, she grabbed the vodka.

"Okay then." May spoke as softly as the music would allow. "I'm sorry we bothered you. We'll head off now."

"Thanks." Noah looked relieved as he opened the door for them.

"You know, I'd have taken those knickers off if you'd asked me. See ya." Noah blushed again as May kissed his cheek and Jess skipped down the steps.

"So what now, Mags?"

"Let's go to the bridge."

May took a large slug of vodka before passing the bottle to Jess. She sipped carefully, pulling a face of disgust as the vodka stung her throat. The two walked arm in arm, towards Archway Bridge.

Chapter 13

"And can I have sixty Marlboro Red and two bottles of Jack Daniels please?" Jess sheepishly asked as she placed four ready meals and two large bars of dairy milk neatly on to the counter.

"£67.40 please." The cashier asked passively.

"How much?"

"Sixty-seven pounds and forty pence. Do you want me to put something back?" The cashier smiled patronisingly.

"No, I can afford it. It's just a bit more than I expected, that's all."

"Oh. Okay. Do you want a bag?"

"No. I've got my own, thanks." I'm not paying for one of those too, Jess thought to herself.

Jess left the mini-mart, and hurriedly made her way home across the estate. She was regretting her decision not to wear her coat, as wisps of cold air caught at her collar. A bright and sunny morning had given way to a chilly afternoon, and the sun seemed to be trying to sneak beneath the horizon without being noticed.

Jess hadn't so much needed to visit the shop, as simply to fetch Mags some essentials. Aside from the ridiculous price of her shopping, she didn't mind being out. The opportunity to get out of the flat and attempt to make sense of matters was more than welcome. She was hardly the perfect house guest, but Mags provided the company that

Jess was sorely missing. She hoped that having Mags around would give her the kick up the backside that she needed to get on with her life again. Every time Jess thought about her stagnation, whether it was her work, her love life or her music, her insides twisted. She could feel the pain of regret turning her one way, whilst the fear of failure yanked her the other as hard as it could. She had found that the best way to avoid it hurting was to completely ignore it. Jess knew that having Mags staying with her would probably force her to face up to her issues. She was dreading it.

As she stepped out of the lift, the sun made a desperate attempt to offer late afternoon warmth as it peeked between the trees in the distance. In doing so, Jess found herself half-blinded by the rays, as they split and shattered on the opaque wired safety-glass balconies. She could hear the scraping of her own footsteps grow faster as she rushed to get back.

"Thank fuck you're back. I'm gasping for a ciggy." Mags shouted from the living room as Jess opened the door.

Mags rushed over to Jess like a puppy greeting a returning owner.

"Marlboro reds." Jess pulled the drink from the bag. "And two bottles of Jack Daniels too."

"Thanks, sweetheart. You're a lifesaver. Smoke?" Mags ripped off the cellophane and pointed the pack at Jess.

"No. I gave up years ago."

"Are you sure? Nobody would blame you."

"I don't, I…" Mags lit a cigarette, and passed it to Jess. "I hate you sometimes, Margaret."

Jess put the cigarette to her lips and took a hefty puff. As soon as she did, she could feel the blood rushing to her head. This was quickly followed by a coughing fit. She eased herself down on to the sofa to regain some composure. Mags sat on the sofa opposite. Eventually, the coughing stopped.

"Are we a little bit out of practice love? I won't offer you again." Mags smiled devilishly.

"I just forgot what it was like. That's all."

"Whatever. While you were out, I worked out how to sort out all of our problems."

Jess laughed, unable to believe that there could be one single idea that could disentangle all of their issues. She pulled on the cigarette, this time with a little more success.

"Go on then. Humour me. What's your big plan, your grand idea?"

"When I've got big issues, I write."

"And?" Jess looked confused.

"No 'and'. That's it!" Mags beamed, hopefully.

"That's it?"

"Trust me. It's catharsis, self-analysis, and probably a load of other shit that costs £150 an hour with a therapist. And if you're anywhere near as good as you used to be, you'll get spotted after a few gigs. You're fucking outstanding."

"I don't do live gigs. I haven't written a song since I left uni. I barely play at all these days. I've got no contacts in the music industry." Jess tried to downplay the idea.

"If only you had someone around you who knew what they were doing." Mags looked around, feigning confusion.

"Come on Mags, it's not that simple."

"It is. Just write." Mags was becoming impatient.

"They won't be any good."

"For fuck's sake, Jess. Nobody ever sings the songs you didn't write."

Jess got up from the sofa and disappeared into the bedroom. Mags poured herself a large glass of Jack Daniels. Within a few seconds Jess had returned with an old notebook and her laptop. She slid them along the coffee table as she sat down again.

"Right then. If we're doing this, then we will be doing it properly. Now, are you going to play that thing, or am I?" She pointed to the guitar on the wall.

"I'm easy, babe." Mags began to beam.

"Can you pour me a glass of that whiskey please Mags, this could be a long evening."

Chapter 14

If you look at a map, the point where Hornsea Lane crosses over the Archway Road looks like any other ordinary, unremarkable road underpass. It is only if you find yourself there, that you quickly discover it is actually anything but ordinary. The bridge itself is a beautiful Victorian cast iron structure that sits astride a leafy cutting. The road through the cutting is busy, and soon finds itself in Holloway, before it starts the crawl in towards Central London.

It is from the top of the bridge that the ordinary is actually elbowed aside by the remarkable though. Even on a relatively cloudy day, it is possible to see the skyscrapers of London standing proudly on the horizon. The capital lays before you in all its glory, looking just like a perfect miniature village.

The locals, however, have a different view. It is often known as suicide bridge, and despite spiked railings, many people over the years have jumped or fallen to their tragic deaths on the road below.

"So, can you explain to me just exactly why we're going to see a bridge at 9 o'clock on a Thursday evening?" Jess asked, as she followed May along the road.

"Like I said, it's where I used to go to think." May shouted over her shoulder, striding ahead.

"It's just a bridge though. What's so special about that?"

May had stopped, and was standing, staring into the distance. Jess was trying to regain her breath. Eventually she caught up, following May's gaze.

"Oh. I see."

The pair stood and looked on silently at the twinkling lights of London, stretching from the almost discernible shapes in windows two or three streets away to the pin-pricks in the buildings in the far distance.

"It's all there, Jess." May spoke without looking away.

"What is?"

"Everything." She paused. "Every bit of life, every human emotion is happening out there, right now. Out there, people will be falling in and out of love. There'll be people dying, while others bring a newborn home for their first night on earth. Somebody will be having the best day of their life. Someone will be kissing a loved one for the last time. Young, old, billionaire, tramp. Anything you can think of, it's out there. Sometimes it helps to find perspective. It's fucked up, really. It's good to remind yourself that whatever is happening to you, everyone else out there is going through all sorts of shit. Good and bad. Knowing that all that is going on, you can't feel alone, can you?"

"I think I get it, Mags." May passed Jess a bottle of beer.

"It makes you feel small, insignificant. I know what I'm really like, Jess. It isn't always what I pretend to be."

"You don't have to tell me all of this, Mags." Jess turned to face her.

"You don't have to listen. I just feel like I can trust you. I'll shut up if you want."

"I don't mind. I clocked there was more to you than you let on in less than ten minutes." Both of them took a large swig of their drinks.

"You know, none of this is actually who I am. It's just me doing what I need to do to survive."

"I know." Jess put her hand on May's.

"By the time I was 18, I was on my own. I had to fight for everything. Making stuff, especially music, was everything. I needed it. It isn't showing off like everyone always thinks. It's just a need to feel like I'm worth something. Some people hate it, but when I'm on stage, I'm doing it, it's happening. I can shut out the world. That's the easy bit. It's the other shit I struggle with."

"You're going to be huge. You really are amazing." Jess smiled sweetly at May.

"Oh, I know. I'm fucking awesome. And you'd *still* be better than me if you'd tried."

Jess laughed. "Where did you see me? I haven't been on stage in years."

"Stage fright?"

"Not really. When I started seeing Nick, it just didn't feel so important."

"It was in my first term at LSMP. They showed us first-years the graduates show reels, so we could see what we were working towards. Yours was the first I saw. I fell in love with you there and then. You really shouldn't have jacked it in."

"I didn't have the passion for it, not like you."

"It isn't passion. I can't fail. That's it. It scares me. I'm not strong enough to deal with that." May took a large glug of vodka.

"I can't imagine anyone being stronger or more fearless than you."

"Really?" May scoffed, unable to hide her incredulity.

An awkward silence sat between the two. Jess didn't know what to say.

"After Greg fucked me off, I had an abortion." May spoke, her voice faltering.

"I beg your pardon?" Jess was unsure if she had heard May properly.

"We'd been seeing each other for a few months, I was just starting my second year at uni. He was twenty years older, but it really didn't bother us. I met him at a gig. He was fucking gorgeous. In the end, he left his wife for me, and we were so happy together. Then, after a couple of months, I fell pregnant. In my mind, even though I'd never thought about it, I quickly got it all planned out. I was ready to jack it all in, just teach piano and be a mum. I imagined this whole bohemian lifestyle. So I told him. I told him I was pregnant. He totally blanked me. I couldn't contact him at all. Within a month, I'd been to visit a clinic. When I told him what I'd done, he went ape-shit. Greg went back to his wife, and I haven't seen him since."

"Oh Mags, you poor darling."

Jess put her arm around May. May's head fell onto Jess' shoulder. May threw her arm around Jess as she heaved in sobs. Tears ran down Jess' cheeks.

"Sometimes, I'd come up here. I'd stand here for hours. I've even thought about jumping."

"Suicide?" Jess asked, disbelieving.

"No. Just on the off-chance I can fly." May went back to looking over London. "I guess so. I don't think I could bring myself to do it."

"Even if it is the only answer, suicide is the wrong answer."

"Oh, I know. It doesn't always feel like that though. Sometimes you just…" May paused.

"Just what? You're not serious, are you?"

"It's crossed my mind. I can't lie. That's all."

"Really?"

"Can we not talk about this, Jess?"

"Sorry Mags, I really didn't…"

"I know. If you've not been there, it isn't easy to get it." May linked her arm into Jessica's. "I don't suppose you'd stop at mine tonight?"

"I guess so." Jess smiled, feeling guilty for pushing her.

"Just don't try to shag me. I don't always do that on a first date. Even if you are cute as fuck." Mags grinned, tears still on her face.

Jess laughed as the two began to walk to the tube station, arm in arm.

Chapter 15

It is sometimes said that there are as many ways to write a song as there are songwriters writing them. There is no hard and fast definitive solution, no 'best way' to write. For most musicians, it is simply a case of discovering what works for them. Some will start with a riff or chord progression, and work backwards, painstakingly piecing together a melody and words from there. Others will start with poetry, finding a tune with the right feel to go with it, working from this point. Some will chop and change between the two. Either way, what tends to follow is a considerable period of nurture, hard work and honing in order to produce a finished song.

There are also a few composers who are barely songwriters at all. The lucky ones. This was the category that May invariably found herself in. She often found that rather than writing music, songs just happened to her. Before she had secured fame and fortune, May would often wake up with fully formed songs in her head. Her only task was little more than that of a scribe, simply writing them down, and polishing them up.

One broadsheet journalist had, in a very positive interview, described her as a musical auteur. She loved this idea at the time, but as she struggled with her demons, the description hung around her neck like an albatross. Every day she found herself staring at the stark white page in front of her, clinging onto her acoustic guitar, praying for anything approaching inspiration. May had tried alcohol and other drugs to assist her, all to little avail.

Jess, on the other hand, had always found writing difficult. For her, it was hard graft from start to finish. Every word, every note was calculated and deliberated over. She hated every second of it, but was always proud of the results. Consequently, she had literally tens of notebooks full of songs in various stages of completion. These days, she rarely found any inclination to write.

"How many demos have we recorded now, chick?" Mags asked in a tobacco roughened voice.

"*I* have recorded nearly thirty. *You* have sat there, getting drunk as a lord, pressing record when I asked, so long as you could be bothered to."

"I've told you before, love, I'm not about the technology, or the nuts and bolts. I have written six songs for you though, and you've hardly been shy about helping me with my booze." Mags smiled at Jess.

"You've literally made me shut out the world. I have had my phone switched off for ages, and my parents probably think I'm dead. I haven't even seen daylight in…" Jess trailed off. "… actually, I don't have any idea exactly how long it has been."

"I'd guess about two weeks. But you've got thirty demos that you didn't have before."

"I suppose so." Jess took a drag on her cigarette. "I've also gained a few vices that I could live without too."

"Hardly worth checking into The Priory for, is it?"

"So then." Jess did her best to ignore Mags, who was quietly giggling to herself. "What do we do now?"

"Keep twelve songs, bin the rest." Mags replied plaintively.

"What?"

"It's tough, but you need to murder your darlings. Be a hard-faced bitch on this. If you can't pick twelve from the rest, then I reckon none of them are worth saving."

"I've just spent weeks on these. I've poured out emotions I didn't know I had and written stories into songs that I would never tell a living soul. I'm not throwing my unused demo songs away." Jess shook her head with incredulity.

"Fine." Mags sat up, looking slightly put out. "You do what you like. They're your songs. Keep them if you have to. But put them on a hard disk and forget they even exist until you're happy with the way the rest of the recordings sound."

"I can do that, if I have to."

Jess and Mags studied the list of demos carefully, each making their cases for their preferred songs. They smoked. They argued. They drank. They shouted and discussed, and finally chose eleven of Mags' list. Jess had to admit that Mags' selection had a delicate and pleasing balance.

"Are you happy with those then?" Mags asked enthusiastically.

"You know what?" Jess smiled. "I am. I think we've got some really good songs here."

"Now pick the one that would be the first single, the one with the shortest intro, and the one that makes you sound sexiest."

"Huh?"

"They are the three demos you need to get bookings and interest." Mags said authoritatively.

"You know, I do know all of this stuff. I did go to LSMP as well." Jess tried to sound less defensive than she felt.

"Fair point love. You've got me bang to rights there, I guess." Mags held up her hands, feigning surrender.

"I'm not saying I know it all. I really am grateful for all of this. I know you've got plenty of experience."

"And an Ivor Novello nomination. Don't forget that." Mags tried to look nonchalant, failing miserably.

Jess blushed. Very quickly, she realised that she was playing down advice from a genuine star.

"Okay. I'm sorry."

"No. Don't be." Mags was defiant.

"I am, though. You're a proper musician, and I'm just an unemployed office manager."

"Fuck off. You're a superstar."

"No, I'm not."

"You will be. Trust me." Mags leant over to Jess and kissed her full on the lips. "There we go. That's the hard bit over. And I think, at the moment, that we're about done here."

"I have got one question though, Mags." Jess whispered into Mags' ear.

"What is it, sweetheart?"

"Can I open the curtains again now?"

Chapter 16

"I'm sorry, I still don't really get it." Nick stood aimlessly staring at the bedroom mirror, combing his hair.

"What? What is it that you don't get?" Jess was sitting on the edge of the bed, rummaging around underneath for her smart shoes.

"Well, you spend one night with May Mornington, and six months later you two are still texting every day and we're on the guest list at the Apollo."

"We just get on. That's all."

Nick turned to Jess as she adjusted her shoes. "Really? You just get on. Okay."

"What's that supposed to mean?" Nick couldn't tell if Jess was being serious.

"Nothing." Nick stood watching as Jess tightened the straps on her dress. "Did you two sleep together?"

"For God's sake, Nick. Not this again."

"It's a reasonable question. You've never really answered it properly."

"What do you want me to tell you? Didn't I give you enough salacious details? Do you want me to lez the story up for you? Tell you what, why don't I ask her if she fancies a threesome?" Even Jess wasn't sure how serious she was being.

"I just want the truth." Nick was becoming dismayed.

"We shared a bed, she gave me a hug, we went to sleep, she woke me up in the morning with a cup of tea and a slice of toast. I've told you all of this."

"I'm sorry. I've never had a girlfriend who was mates with one of the darlings of the NME before." Nick backtracked, trying not to appear jealous.

Nick and Jess looked sharp and beautiful as they left the flat. Instinctively, Jess reached out for Nick's arm. He shrugged it away without even looking, before Jess made another, more determined attempt. Eventually, their arms entwined as they wandered silently towards the tube. A short wait, and a change of trains later, and the couple were still entangled as they exited Hammersmith underground station into the rain-soaked street.

Hammersmith, and more specifically the Hammersmith Apollo have been the epicentre of mainstream music in London since the 1950s. The beautiful, sweeping art déco fronted building was originally thrown up in the early 1930s as The Gaumont Cinema. By the 1960s and 70s, it was *the* destination to play in London. Heavy metal, glam rock and even jazz graced the stage of The Odeon, as it was then known. By the mid-90s, it was renamed as The Apollo, and appeared on the normal UK tour circuit. Everyone who was anyone relished the chance to appear there. In the early 2000s it became familiar to a wider audience, as the venue for many BBC comedy shows. Despite the commercial nature, it is still considered by many to be one of the most revered music venues in London.

The sequence of events that had seen May Mornington find herself at the top of the bill here had been almost as convoluted. Fortune had inadvertently put her in exactly the right place on a number of occasions, and May had taken full advantage. Shortly after signing with

Impact, she had been busy recording her debut album when Jakki Strong, a long forgotten icon of 80s pop, had heard her singing from the other side of a studio door as she was on her way out. On the strength of this, Jakki invited May to open for her as she went on a comeback British tour, the showpiece culmination of which was to be two triumphant nights at the Apollo. After three weeks of average ticket sales at provincial venues, May Mornington's first single had found itself being placed onto the 'A' playlist for BBC Radio 1, 2 and 6 music, and most commercial stations. A hastily cobbled together video and minimal publicity somehow still managed to propel her squarely into the middle of the UK top 40. Suddenly, Jakki Strong was relegated to becoming little more than May Mornington's support act. This unfortunate, and entirely unintentional upstaging was not well received by Ms Strong, who quickly made the decision to cancel the remainder of her tour with little fanfare, citing family issues and emotional stress. In reality, poor ticket sales had left the tour barely viable. Impact records, not wishing to waste an opportunity to make money, set about re-selling the big city venues as May Mornington gigs, offering up showcase opportunities for local acts. Three months later, May had managed to score a UK top 10 when her follow-up single was featured heavily in a clothes advert, and her album began selling in reasonable, if less than earth shattering quantities. She had also managed to sell almost 7000 tickets over two nights at the Apollo. Tonight was to be the first of these. May Mornington was rapidly becoming nervous and excited in equally large measures. Despite an open invitation to join the bill, Jakki Strong was nowhere to be seen.

"Evening guys. Can I see your tickets, please?" A tall, suited doorman asked in a firm but friendly manner.

"Yeah, sure. Here you go." Jess handed over the two tickets.

"Ah. Guest list tickets. Miss Mornington has requested that you two join her backstage. Would you like to follow me, please?" The doorman mumbled something unintelligible into a radio and gestured for Jess and Nick to follow.

They were led through corridor after corridor. As Jess and Nick approached the dressing rooms, they could hear May before they saw her.

"Can't he just put up with normal Pepsi? I just wish he'd stop being such a precious little cock."

"He says he can't drink it, but I'll try. He's tricky to talk to at the moment though." Mickey shouted, surrounded by musicians and chaos.

Mickey George, May's middle-aged keyboard player, was, as ever, trying to keep everybody happy. Right now, he was failing dramatically. It seemed that whenever he attempted to pour oil on troubled water, May would be right behind him, waiting with a petrol bomb and a lighter.

"He's only a guitarist, just tell him to fuck off. We'll just ask someone in the audience. A trained monkey could play his part." An obviously stressed out May turned to the door. Her face beamed when she saw Jessica. "Jess! Thank fuck you're here."

May ran over to her and threw her arms around her. She held her tightly and rested her head against Jessica's.

"Is everything alright, Mags?" Nick asked.

"I'm fine. But that skinny prick over there is making a fuss because he's not got Pepsi Max." May pointed at a wiry-looking musician sitting on a sofa.

"Just talk to him calmly Mags, he's probably got reasons." Jess tried to calm May down.

"Fine. The fuckwit."

"What's his name?" Nick asked.

May looked back blankly, half-shrugging her shoulders.

Mickey stepped in. "Oh, for fuck's sake Mags, it's Brandon. He's been on tour with us for the last six weeks."

"Just go and talk to him." Jess urged gently. "I bet there is a perfectly reasonable explanation."

May strode over to him purposefully, looking ready to start a fight.

"Calmly!" Jess shouted after her.

May stood talking to him. As she did so, her body language softened from confrontational to submissive. After a few minutes, May smiled, rested a friendly hand on his shoulder before squeezing gently and walking away.

"See? Not that bad, was it?" Jess smiled smugly, pleased that her advice had worked.

"He's diabetic. Are you always right?" May grinned back.

Nick looked across to May with a perfectly deadpan face. "Usually."

Jess pushed Nick's arm whilst May and Nick were laughing at her.

"Go on you two, grab yourselves a drink. I'll be back in a minute, I need to find my drummer."

May disappeared into the corridor with Mickey and Brandon, as they hunted for a percussionist.

Chapter 17

Almost immediately after they finished the demos, Jessica became overwhelmed by a growing and insatiable urge to sleep. Even the minuscule walk from the lounge to the bedroom had suddenly become hard work, as she wearily plodded to her room, with legs almost as heavy as her eyes.

Jess' head sank deep into the pillow, and as the rhythmic sound of adrenalin-filled blood pumping in her ears began to subside, sleep quickly began to consume her. It could have been minutes or days later when she was stirred to half-awakening by May playing Jessica's songs in the living room. She drifted back off, as beautiful music carried itself into her ears. She awoke several times. Each time she was caressed back into sleep with a soothing lullaby provided by May Mornington.

"Are you Dead, Jess?" May shouted impatiently.

She leant over and idly prodded the limp, corpse-like shape in the bed. Jess awoke with a scream as May's face hovered above hers, mere inches away. Out of reflex, May screamed back.

"What on earth are you doing?" Jess screeched hysterically.

"I was getting lonely and hungry." May squawked, confused and scared.

"Goodness, Mags. Please don't do that again. I thought I was about to have a heart attack. How long have I been asleep for?"

"About seventeen hours."

Jess pulled herself up to a sitting position. May sat on the bed next to her. Slowly, Jessica's brain began to re-boot properly.

"Crikey. That long?"

"Give or take. I've been rattling around since about twenty-past five. Couldn't sleep."

"Right. What do we do now then, Mags?"

"Well, you get up, have a shower, and make us breakfast, and then you can start getting in touch with promoters and A&R people."

"Surely I could just speak to your people at Impact, couldn't I?" Jess tailed off.

Mags was shaking her head. Her face twisted as she sucked air between her teeth.

"You could. But I'd be wary. They're a bunch of money grabbing cunts."

"Sorry?" Jess was taken aback by May's abrupt language.

"You heard. I've been alright. I can look after myself. They'd eat you for breakfast. I mean, call them if you want. They'll probably sign you. You're talented and pretty and just about young enough for them to want to screw you. Just remember that when they pass you over to Tom James in the A&R department, that he's a sleazy little shit-bag. Don't trust him as far as you can throw him."

"Oh, right."

Jess had so many questions, but didn't dare ask them.

"In fact, you probably should call them. Arrange a meeting. Just keep your wits about you if you do."

"Can't you help me? In fact, can't you manage me?" Jess asked.

"I don't exist anymore, do I?" May leant into Jess' shoulder. "I'm sorry, sweetheart. I can teach you everything I know, and I can try to give you my best advice. You can learn from all of my many, many mistakes, but I can't run your career for you. I'm resigned to a quietly anonymous existence from now on."

"So what *are* you going to do? I don't suppose you're going to want to stay here forever."

"What's this? Squeeze me dry and fuck me off?" May laughed.

"Oh God, no. You can stay forever if you want."

"I know, darling. I was only joking with you." May rested her hand on Jessica's. "I'll go when the time's right, don't you worry about that."

The two smiled and looked at each other before Jess jumped up assertively.

"Righty oh. Cup of tea then?"

"That'd be ace. Thanks chick."

As Jess bumped and banged around in the kitchen, May sat herself down, kicking her feet onto the coffee table, one by one. She reached into her bra, and pulled out her cigarettes before lighting one and taking a large, luxuriant puff. As she did, Jess returned with two cups of tea.

"Seriously though, do you really think I am better off steering clear of Impact?"

"No. Fuck it. Don't let my opinions make your mind up. In fact…"

May grabbed Jessica's laptop and began typing.

"What are you doing, Mags?"

May didn't respond, but kept typing. After a moment, she reached across and snatched Jess' mobile phone from her hand. She tapped in a number and threw it back to Jess.

"There you go. It's ringing." May giggled.

"Who am I calling?" Jess mouthed at May, eyes filled with terror and confusion.

"Hello. Impact records. Artist and Repertoire Department. How can I help you?"

Chapter 18

The green room was lined with tables, covered with neatly lined up rows of bottles of alcohol. Subdued lighting and subtle decor made the place feel calm and civilised. Art déco fittings added an impressive grandeur to the room. The dull hum of a band could be heard through soundproofed walls. A member of the theatre staff busied herself with straightening the cushions on the large sofas, but other than that, the room was deserted.

Meanwhile, May Mornington was drawing her encore to a close. An audience of thousands were hanging on her every word and note. The auditorium was filled with a visceral crackle of energy. May could feel it too. As she got to the keyboard break before the final chorus of the last song, she looked across to Mickey. His concentration-etched face was glistening with sweat, as he bashed away for all he was worth. Dark patches under his arms had permeated through his shirt and onto his jacket.He briefly looked up, winking. May smiled warmly to herself, delighting in watching the master-sorcerer in the act of making magic. She took a deep, quivering breath, before launching herself into the final chorus.

"Okay. I have to admit that you're right. She really is something special." Nick shouted to Jess as they left the auditorium.

"Well, I did say." Jess smirked back. "We're invited to the after-party. You don't mind going in for a drink or two, do you?"

"No. Not at all. I'd love to see her again. Even if it's just to say she was wonderful."

"Tyler said he might be there too."

"Oh, cool. I can't remember the last time we met up for a drink." Nick's face brightened.

"I thought you'd like that."

Jess led Nick by the hand through the crowds as they left. When they finally got to the green room, they could see an ebullient Mickey, holding onto an enormous glass of brandy. Mickey was now wearing a fresh pale pink shirt with a large white collar, and jeans that seemed to be too long for his legs. He waddled over past the selected few, full of excitement.

"Hello darlin'. How was that for you? Help yourselves to drinks."

Nick went over to the table to find some beer.

"You were absolutely fantastic up there tonight. It was great to see you playing again."

"Thanks love. It's all down to May. I'd never tell her, but she really is a bit special. Makes me look good!"

"Where is she?" Jess looked around the room as she spoke.

"I think she went to get changed. I reckon she sweats almost as much as me under those lights."

"Come off it Mickey. I doubt there are many people in the world who sweat as much as you on stage." Jake appeared again, apparently out of nowhere.

"Alright Jakey, me old china. How's it going, guvna'?"

"I'm good, mate. Not as good as you, though. You guys were incredible tonight."

"Cheers, boss. Oh, have you met Jess?"

"Briefly. We met once at The Dublin Castle." Jake smiled and shook Jessica's hand. "Can I get you a drink?"

"No, my boyfriend has just gone to get one." Jess smiled back regretfully.

"Another time, maybe. Have you seen May?"

"I think she's gone to get changed." Jess replied.

"No, have you seen her, she's over there."

Jake pointed towards the door. May was standing in the doorway. She was wearing a black fitted cocktail dress and looked elegant and sophisticated. Her eyes darted around the room. Eventually, her gaze found Jessica. All of a sudden, her face came alive. She seemed to glide across the room towards them.

"Well? What do you think?" May held her arms out towards Jess.

"The concert or the dress? Both are just perfect."

May grabbed Jessica and kissed her before holding on to her as tightly as she could. Mickey began to talk to her.

"You know what, Mags?" He said, sloshing brandy around his glass. "Over the last few years, I've pointed out every bum note, and every missed lyric you've made. Tonight love, you were absolutely brilliant. Bang on the money." He took a swig of brandy. "Now don't make me say it again!"

"Aw. Thanks Mickey. Coming from you, that's high praise. High praise indeed. You were pretty good too." May put her hand on Mickey's shoulder.

"And that frock looks smashing too. I tell you, if I was thirty years younger…"

May quietly and slowly moved her hand away from Mickey's shoulder, and back to her side. Nick elbowed his way between Mickey and Jess, holding two beers in each hand.

"Sorry I was a while, I got talking to Tyler."

"Is he over there?" May asked. "I haven't seen him yet."

"Yeah. He's chatting to your guitarist."

"Oh, cool. I don't suppose he's still in touch with Curtis? A couple of grams of something would be just the ticket right now."

"How many times Mags? Stay away from that stuff, or it'll mess you up." Jake urged, sounding like a protective father.

"You'll be lucky. Curtis has been, erm, working away for the last few months." Nick responded.

"That's a pity. He's sound as a pound. When's he back in London?"

"About three years, maybe sooner with good behaviour."

"Shame. I'll just have to get pissed instead. Are you guys joining me?"

Jess looked on disapprovingly. Mags grabbed Mickey's brandy and necked it in one go.

"Jess and me need to head off after this beer. Sorry." Nick threw Jess a look as he spoke.

"Don't forget, you're playing here tomorrow as well, Mags."

Jessica faced Mags as Nick began to lead her away.

"It's alright. It's only the record label guys on the guest list tomorrow. I'll be fine."

"Don't worry about her Jess." Mickey smiled. "Me and Jake will look after her."

"I don't need looking after. I am a big girl."

"You won't be needing us then, will you?" Jake smiled.

"Fine." May's shoulders dropped as she spoke. "Can somebody bring me a bottle of Tequila?"

Chapter 19

"Are you really going to be wearing that for your appointment?" May asked as she reclined on Jess' sofa, reading a magazine.

"Why? What's wrong with it? I look nice and smart." Jess asked, straightening the lapels of her navy blue trouser suit.

"You look like you got lost on your way to the HR department."

"I don't think there's anything the matter with it." Jess defended herself.

"Oh come on darling, look at yourself. It's a chat with the Impact A&R department, not the businesswoman of the year awards."

"It's only about the music, not my appearance."

"Okay, Jess." May smiled as she spoke, hiding between the advertising pages. "If that's what you want to believe."

"Anyway, what happened to not encouraging Tom James? I thought you said he was a lecherous old man."

"He is. Don't try to face up to it, though. Use it, use him to your advantage."

"What do you mean?"

"If he thinks he stands a chance with you, then he'll do whatever he can to get some. He doesn't need to know that it's going nowhere, and you know all about him. If he thinks he'll end up in your knickers, then he's pretty likely to do whatever you want."

"That's not really fair though, is it?"

"No, but neither is the fact that they make the rules. It's a screwed up world, designed by, and run for men. Not all men are wankers, but most wankers are men. And if we're honest, the old phrase is all wrong."

"What phrase?" Jess asked.

"Sex sells. Bullshit. Sex doesn't actually sell at all. The *idea* of sex, the possibility of sex, the promise of sex is what sells. What scumbags like Tom don't realise is that he's destined to be the sucker who is buying it."

"I don't want him to think I've got no morals."

May laughed. "You really are an innocent, aren't you? Just let him *think* he can have you. Flirt a bit. Just make sure you get in, get signed, and get gone before he has a crack at you. You'll be lucky to keep your breakfast down if he does. You saw the email he sent. The one where he says he needs to meet you to 'get a feel' of what you're like in person. The filthy prick. You keep your wits about you."

"Oh Mags, why can't you just come with me?"

May looked up from her music magazine. "Because a famous popstar who was announced as dead less than a month ago isn't going to arouse suspicion if she's spotted walking down to her own record label office in Soho, is she? For a clever girl, you really do say some daft shit."

"I just wanted you with me. I know it was a stupid suggestion, I'm not *that* silly."

Jess looked at May with dismay and frustration, yet it was Jess who began laughing first.

"Sorry, sweetheart." May giggled back. "You're just so fucking naïve sometimes."

"I'll go and get changed. What do you reckon I should wear then, O wise one?"

"Something that shows that you've got great tits and a cute backside."

Jess disappeared to the bedroom. May returned to reading an article about mid-priced guitars in her magazine.

Jessica had a wardrobe that was filled with many plain and functional clothes. She wasn't unfashionable, but she didn't tend to do sexy very often, and had very little need for elegance. It had been months since she had gone out properly, and as she stared at the rows of clothes in front of her, nothing seemed to be right for the occasion. If she was being honest with herself, Jess had no idea what clothes would be suitable. She rifled back and forth between the garments before begrudgingly admitting defeat.

"Mags?" She shouted through to the lounge.

"What now?" May shouted back, barely looking up from her magazine.

"Can you come and give us a hand? I'm struggling a bit in here."

May appeared at the door with a delighted grin plastered across her face. "Go back in there and sit down, I'll give you a shout when I'm done."

"Don't you dare dress me up like a hooker."

May smirked, feigning innocence. "As if I would. Oh, before you go, have you got any scissors?"

"No. Not for you." Jess answered sternly.

"Joking. Honest"

Jess busied herself with the magazine, sitting neatly on the sofa like a patient in a doctors' surgery waiting room. She didn't dare think too hard about what outfit May would choose, but committed herself to wearing it, whatever it might be.

"I'm ready for you, sweetheart."

Jess plodded to the bedroom nervously. On the bed was a tiny white, ripped sideless vest, and a pair of flared jeans. May nodded and smiled hopefully whilst Jess stared in disbelief.

"I take it you've got a half-decent bra on."

"I hope so. Looks like I'll need it with that vest. I'm sure that the sides of that top didn't used to be ripped."

"I've improved it."

"Oh, of course. What else am I going to wear then? Where's the rest of the outfit?"

"What, like shoes and stuff?"

"I meant a jumper, or a jacket. I'll freeze my boobs off out there."

"Jessica, you know that art is suffering."

"That is as may be, but pneumonia is pneumonia. I'm wearing my green corduroy jacket. It is quite fitted, very feminine."

"Fine, but take it off when you get into his office. At least it's not a cagoule or a fleece, I suppose."

Jess wriggled into the outfit and found herself staring at herself in the mirror. Her wavy brown hair nestled gently against her collar, and some dark, yet subtle eye makeup only added to her natural prettiness. She was pleasantly surprised at how attractive she looked.

"Do I look okay?" She asked, without turning to May.

"You'll do. I'd try my luck with you. Now, you get that pretty little arse in gear before you're late. You've got a record deal to get."

Chapter 20

Hampstead is a pretty, leafy suburb in North-London. Partially hemmed in by the parkland of Hampstead Heath, huge numbers of spacious, beautiful villas and townhouses were built in the second half of the 19th century shortly after the arrival of the railways. These were rapidly filled by the Victorian bohemian elite, who turned Hampstead into an enclave of intelligentsia. Between the wars, it once again became a hot spot of culture, thought and creativity, as the great and good fleeing revolutionary Russia and Nazi Germany descended upon the relative safety of suburban London. Since those days, Hampstead and its surrounding areas has been been called home by scores of world renowned film stars, writers and musicians alike. Even today, the boutique shops of Hampstead high street are often frequented by the rich and famous of London society.

As Jess and Nick walked along the tree-lined avenue, early evening summer sun fell and scattered in small clumps between the leaves. Jess was wearing a pretty, burgundy coloured cocktail dress, whilst Nick had opted for trainers, track suit bottoms and a purple t-shirt.

"It's a townhouse in Belsize Park Jess, not bloody Buckingham Palace." Nick mumbled grumpily, fiddling with his mobile phone.

"I don't care. It's a housewarming party, isn't it? I just think it's right to make a bit of an effort. What if there are some other famous people there?"

"What if there are? They won't give a stuff that I'm wearing a polo instead of a shirt and tie. It's only Mags. Hardly Sunday lunch with the Windsors, is it?"

Nick and Jess had found themselves at a point in their relationship where they could, and often would, happily bicker about anything. Unchecked, this would regularly continue almost indefinitely.

"I really think that is important to try and leave a positive impression. I don't want anybody thinking that we're a pair of slobs." Jess was becoming irate.

Nick barely looked up from his phone as he spoke. "They can think what they like. I don't mind Mags, but I'm only really here for you."

"Goodness. Thank you. I'm so glad you joined me." Jess said sarcastically, turning her head away as she did. "I just hope you're going to be a bit more engaging when you get inside. Mags did actually say she was looking forward to seeing you. When you're in a mood like this, heaven knows why."

"Well, I hope you're going to cheer up a bit when we get there."

"Me cheer up? You're the one who's been glued to his phone since we got of the tube."

"I told you. It's work." Nick looked up. "Hold on, is that Mickey over there?"

The door of a mid-terrace townhouse was ajar. Mickey was showing a level of manual dexterity that was easily on a par with his musical ability, simultaneously shouting into his mobile phone whilst managing to hold a large cigar and a glass of brandy. Somehow he was still able to give Jess and Nick a thumbs up.

"Alright darlin'. 'Allo Nicky boy. How's it going?" He mouthed, obviously trying not to be heard on his phone.

"We're good." Nick said. "We'll catch up later, mate."

"Watch out when you go in. There's a Gallagher brother in there somewhere. He seems okay at the moment though, but you know what they're like. One wrong move, and whoosh, he'll be off like a rocket." Mickey gestured towards his phone, before turning away and continuing his conversation.

Jess and Nick walked through the door and into a surprisingly spacious hallway. Black-and-white floor tiles made a striking impression. A large houseplant stood in one corner. Smooth jazz music appeared to be coming from nowhere, and small groups of well-dressed people were gathered in clumps, drinking what looked like champagne. Jess stuck her head around the first door she saw and found herself looking into a plush and comfy living room with a ridiculously large television. More people were gathered, standing, talking, laughing. Jess didn't recognise anybody.

Nick took Jess by the arm, urging her into the kitchen. A large, stylish open-plan kitchen-diner, backed with skylights and bi-fold doors lay in front of them. The large granite topped island was surrounded by more people drinking from champagne flutes and eating small blobs of food on top of tiny little crackers.

Tyler, wearing a plain white shirt and skinny blue trousers, emerged from the crowd. "Nick, Jess. Long time no see. How are you doing?"

"We're good, bro. I wasn't expecting you to be here."

"You know me, never one to miss out on a party." The two men embraced before Tyler kissed Jess on the cheek. "Wow Jess, you look amazing. You're putting him to shame. Let me grab you two a drink."

Jess turned to Nick and whispered. "See, I told you to dress up."

"There's not much I can do about it now, is there?"

Tyler returned, holding two large champagne flutes. He passed them to Nick and Jess.

"Just try to go steady with the glasses, they're only rented. May's manager will kill you if you break one."

"I think we can manage, but I'm sure she'd be cool if we did." Jess took a quick sip. "Where is she then?"

"Who? Mags?"

"No, the previous homeowner." Jess responded sarcastically. "Of course Mags."

"She went upstairs about twenty minutes ago. Haven't seen her since."

"She could have just gone to the loo." Nick offered, unhelpfully.

"Perhaps you might want to go and have a look for her, Jess. She has been gone a while."

"I suppose so." She responded, hesitantly.

Jess walked away with the nagging feeling that she had been dismissed from the conversation. She stepped up the ornate wooden staircase. As she reached the top, she could see that one of the bedroom doors was ajar. Without thinking, she pushed it open. There in front of her was May, sitting on the floor in a flowing cream summer dress. Her head was resting in her hands, while her elbows were resting on her knees.

"Are you alright, Mags?" Jess asked cautiously.

"Jess?" Mags looked up. She seemed subdued. "Thank God it's you."

"What's up?"

"Nothing. I just needed a bit of time out."

"Really? Party girl May Mornington, looking for a break?"

May laughed in dismay. "Yeah. Really. I guess."

"So, are you going to tell me what's really up?"

"Do I have to?"

"No, we can just sit here if you like."

"So I have to, then."

May looked across to Jess, who was sitting patiently on the bed. She clambered to her feet and sat herself next to Jess.

"Over a year on the road. I've barely been home. And then I come back to this new place."

"It's beautiful though." Jess said.

"Oh, I know. It's fucking incredible. But it doesn't feel like mine. The rent-a-crowd downstairs, it's all rubbish. Mickey, Ty, and you. Possibly Jake as well. Maybe even a couple of my neighbours. That would have done me. Instead, I get this seminar of music business suits descending on me, all talking about growth markets and social media penetration. They're all just lotus-eaters. It's bullshit."

"You can't hide up here all day, can you?"

"Why not? It's my house, isn't it?"

"Yes, but it's your party too. I'm willing to bet that there are some wonderful people downstairs. Mickey says he's seen a Gallagher."

"If I go downstairs, I'll probably end up getting hammered and making a prick of myself, *again*."

"Fine. Then I'll join you."

"What?" May asked, confused.

"If you have to consider someone else, perhaps you'll think a bit more about your actions."

"How do you mean? How is that gonna work?"

"Well, every time you have a drink, I will too. Every time you go outside for a cigarette, I will too. We'll even go to the loo together if you want."

"You don't smoke though."

"I will tonight."

"What about Nick?" May asked.

"What about him? He was being a pain, anyway."

"Alright then." May smiled devilishly. "What if I play a few songs on the piano in the kitchen?"

"Oh, erm. I don't know about that." Jess could feel the plan beginning to backfire spectacularly already.

"Just a few songs. I've always wanted to see you play live."

"But I'll be rubbish. I haven't practiced or anything."

"Play a couple of songs for me, and I'll do it."

Jess took a large gulp of air. "Go on then. Just this once."

Chapter 21

Jess reached out and placed her finger on the intercom buzzer. She could see that her own hand was shaking. It didn't surprise her. She couldn't remember the last time she had been this nervous. She found herself taking a cursory glance at the street around her. After weeks in virtual isolation, the crowds of people in the sun-bleached Soho street felt intimidating. She pressed the button.

A tinny, disembodied voice eventually responded. "Hello, can I help?"

"Oh Hi. It's Jessica Vaughan. I've got an appointment with Tom James at 2pm."

"Come on up."

Jessica edged nervously up the steep, narrow stairs. A grubby, pale brown carpet seemed to be squashed and dirty on each tread. The handrail looked and felt as though it had been painted a dozen times. At the top of the stairs, the staircase opened out into a small reception area.

"Hello Miss Vaughan. I'll let Tom know that you're here."

The receptionist was a small young woman with a bleached blond ponytail, and a face so fresh it looked as though she had barely left school. She tapped away at her computer efficiently. Jess sat and looked around the waiting room. On the walls were photographs of musicians. None were as successful as May. Her picture sat behind the receptionist.

Somehow, the picture didn't quite look right. It looked so forced, so staged. Jess found herself staring, but thought no more of it. Half a dozen badly gloss-painted doors seemed to come from the waiting room. The whole place looked tatty. After a few moments, one of the doors opened. At the door stood a tall older man with smart hair and a smarter suit.

"Hi Jess, it's great to meet you." He smiled broadly and offered a chunky hand.

"You too, Mr James." She shook back. His handshake was firm, but slightly clammy.

"Oh, call me Tom. There's no need for formalities, is there?"

Tom held the door open for Jess and gestured towards a plush chair. His office was far smarter and modern than she had expected. Jess took her coat off and sat down.

"Okay, Tom."

"Right. Shall we get straight down to business?" He paused. "I've listened to your demos. I like them. They're nice."

"Thanks."

Tom looked through his paperwork. "Have I got this right?"

"What's that?"

"You were friends with May Mornington?"

"Yes, that's right. Well, acquaintances really, I suppose."

"It was me that signed her. One of our A&R scouts referred her to me. She was definitely one of a kind." He smiled.

"You can say that again." Jess giggled.

"I've been doing this for nearly twenty years, and I could probably do another twenty without finding anybody with anything like her level of talent. Everything she touched was doused in brilliance. And her sound, her songs, were always so instantly recognisable. You know, much of that was down to my guidance."

"Was it really?" Jess tried to catch her own disbelieving smile.

"Now, your work." He looked at his notes.

"Yes?"

"It's proficient. You have a pleasant voice."

"Thanks."

"Your songs though…"

"Yes?"

"A bit twee perhaps, not exactly brilliant. Don't get me wrong, they are good, but they're nothing special."

"Oh." Jess said, crestfallen.

"This one…" He pointed a remote control at a speaker. "If this is your standard, then I really don't know what we can do with you. Sorry. Perhaps that's a bit too strong. I'm sure we can use you one way or another, but I really don't know if we can offer exactly what you were expecting. "

The two of them sat listening in an awkward silence. Jess, who had grown accustomed to hating the sound of her singing voice, was listening to the beauty of one of the songs that May had penned. She wasn't interested in the singing. Tom pulled faces of exaggerated disappointment. Inside Jess was on fire with anger, disbelief, devastation and confusion. This idiot clearly didn't understand a word of what he was talking about, yet at this moment, it felt as though her entire future seemed to lay wholly in his hands.

"Oh, I see." Jess mumbled.

"Okay, you're in your late twenties. I'm guessing that this is pretty much last chance saloon for you, isn't it?" Tom stood up and stepped from behind his desk.

"I guess."

"I'm not saying you don't stand a chance in the music business…" He stood behind her, starting to breathe more heavily. "And I know you are a pretty girl now, but you're rapidly running out of opportunities, Jess."

"Do you think I'm wasting my time?" Jess asked, as she could already feel her skin beginning to crawl.

She was pretty sure of what was about to follow. It was then that she felt his right hand on her shoulder. His left hand stroked her hair. Already she felt sick.

"No. Not at all. But if we're going to make a star of you, then I think that you're going to need me to give you some very close mentoring." He leant down to whisper in her ear. "Do you understand what I'm saying, honey?"

For a second, Jess froze. Everything that she had feared, everything that May had warned her of, was happening. As quickly as she could, she found her composure.

"I think so, Tom." Jess said firmly.

"So, are you in? Would you like me to mould you?"

"Hmm. Let me see." Jess shook Tom's hands away. "How about no? How about you get your horrible, sweaty hands away from me, and go and find a rock to die under? If I'm expected to massage your minuscule manhood to massage your even smaller ego just so you will give me a record deal that makes me the square root of nothing every month, you can forget it."

"I'm sorry, Jess…"

"Don't you dare sorry me. May warned me about you. I didn't believe that she wasn't exaggerating. I do now. Now give me a good reason why my next phone call shouldn't be to the Metropolitan Police?" Jess was still getting angrier.

"I just. I. I'm…" Tom was lost for words.

"You are no better than something I'd scrape off my shoe. What's more, I feel sorry for you. Sorry that such a pathetic excuse for a human is allowed to abuse his position. You know what? I'm going to take my songs to a label that looks after their artists."

"Good luck finding one of those." Tom sneered, now feeling braver, hiding behind his desk on the other side of his office.

"Really? You want to play that game?" Tom had broken into an embarrassed laugh. "Oh, I'm sorry, Mr Big Shot. Do you find something funny?"

"No." Tom tried to stifle his laugh.

She marched over towards him. "Oh. Because here's the punchline."

Jess pulled her hand into a fist and punched him as hard as she could on the nose. It cracked as she did, and blood began to pour from it immediately.

"I think you've bust my nose. I'm going to sue you, you little slag."

"I wouldn't do that if I was you." Jess turned, grabbed her coat from the back of the chair, and walked out.

"Is everything alright, Miss Vaughan?" The receptionist asked, trying not to sound as though she was prying.

"Yeah. I'm fine. Do yourself a favour though. Go and find a company that doesn't employ misogynistic animals like him. Get out before he tries it on with you too."

Jess stormed down the stairs and stood in the street. She looked down at her hand. The middle knuckle of her right hand was swollen and bloody. Her hands were now shaking uncontrollably. Behind her, she heard the door open and close again. She turned to see the receptionist.

"Are you alright, Miss Vaughan?"

"I think so. Call me Jess though. How about you?"

"I suppose." She smiled. "He looks at me sometimes, and I know exactly what he's thinking. Sometimes he'll touch my arms, it's nothing really, but he leaves his hand there a second or two longer than I'm comfortable with. He makes me feel awkward."

"But that place is your job. Is it wise to walk away from somewhere just because of that?

"It's only a job, innit? I don't need that sort of thing, do I? My name is Keeley, by the way."

"Nice to meet you. I don't suppose you would mind walking with me to the tube station please?"

"Of course I will, Jess."

"Thank you, Keeley."

The two women headed towards the underground station together.

Chapter 22

May Mornington stood in her kitchen holding an expensive looking acoustic guitar. Mickey George sat next to her on a dining room chair in front of an electric piano. Gathered around them were twenty or so of the Hampstead elite, mingled in with some of May's actual friends and label-mates. Beyond them were another two dozen people, apparently belonging to the record label, the touring company and the distributors. Most of those seemed more interested in the champagne than the music. May couldn't care less. She was happily singing a mixture of her songs and cover versions, exuding beauty, talent and confidence. Jess was standing next to Nick, near to the front of the crowd, singing along without a care in the world.

"Keep it down a bit, Jess. People are looking." Nick whispered in Jessica's ear.

"I'm having fun. Perhaps you might be able to remember that." Jess whispered back.

"For God's sake. There are famous people here. I think that girl by the fridge was in Eastenders."

"Why don't you go and stand next to her then? Oh, that's right, you decided that it was a good idea to dress like you've come around to do the bloody garden."

Jess scowled to herself and returned to singing along with May. Nick stood next to her, emotionless. After a couple of minutes, Tyler, who had been standing to Nick's other side, tapped him on the shoulder, and pulled him away towards the champagne.

"And now, while I go and get myself a drink or three, I'd like you all to welcome my best friend to the stage. I say stage, I know it's the kitchen. Just give her a bit of love. Jess, sweetheart, you're on."

Emotions and thoughts rifled through her head, as they always did before a gig. Jess couldn't remember the last time she had played live. It had always been something that she endured, rather than enjoyed. She'd been one of three siblings, all of whom had been musical. Tim, her eldest brother, had been a trombonist in various big bands and concert orchestras, and had toured much of the world with one band or another. Her older sister Charlotte sang and played in a popular covers band with her husband and sister-in-law. Jess had spent her entire childhood surrounded by music and musical instruments. It was no surprise to anybody when she aced all the entrance exams and made the move from a tiny village near Oxford to the busy heart of South London to study music. Playing had always been second nature for Jess. With singing, however, Jess had always struggled. It didn't matter how many times she heard it, or how many people told her how beautiful it was, she hated the way she sounded. Countless lessons meant that she knew everything there was to know about technique, yet she would have been far happier never to have to sing in public again. She had always found herself agonising over criticism, and ignoring praise. In the end, she'd just stopped bothering to try. Yet here she was, shuffling reluctantly towards the stage.

She sat down to the piano, adjusted the microphone stand and cleared her throat.

"Hi." She said, meekly. "Would anyone mind if I played a little bit of David Bowie?"

The crowd mumbled approval. Jess stretched her fingers and began to play. From the opening bars of Absolute Beginners to the momentary silence following the final chord, Jess was note perfect, comfortably matching May for talent. As the gathered crowd clapped and cheered, Jess scanned the audience. May and Mickey were in tears, and Tyler was smiling broadly, clapping. She scoured back and forth. Nick seemed to have vanished.

May walked back to the makeshift stage and held Jess tightly.

"Have you seen Nick?" Jess asked in hushed tones.

"I think he went into the garden on his phone, love. Fuck him. Why don't me and you do a couple of songs together?"

"Oh goodness, I don't know about that." Jess' eyes darted nervously around the room.

"Repeat after me: Fuck him." May put her hands on Jessica's shoulders.

"Yes, Mags. Fuck him." She smiled uncertainly.

"Just stand there, between me and Mickey, and sing along."

"Yes, Mags."

"And don't you dare upstage me again." May laughed. "I'm joking. I've waited years to see you do that. I can die happy now."

May kissed a nervous-looking Jessica on the forehead before launching into another song, this time with her best friend on backing vocals.

Chapter 23

May was leaning out of the balcony window smoking a cigarette when she heard the door of the flat opening and then slamming shut. At first she gave it no thought, preferring to finish her Marlboro before going to check it out. She returned to the living room, fully expecting to see Jess bouncing around, full of the joys of spring. Instead, the room was exactly as it had been before, except for two neatly lined up trainers on the shoe rack. May wandered around the flat, looking for any other sign as to the whereabouts of Jessica. She pushed open the bedroom door. Jess was laying there with her head buried in the pillow.

"What's the matter, sweetheart?" May asked as tenderly as she could.

"Just piss off and leave me alone." Jess spat angrily.

"Why? Come on, tell me what's up?"

"I don't want to talk about it."

"Perhaps if we talk about it, you'll feel better."

"It's not going to change anything."

"Please, Jess. Talk to me."

May brushed the hair away from Jessica's face, still buried deep in her pillow. Then she pulled gently at her shoulder, trying to turn her over. As she did, she could see that Jessica had been crying. Her eye make-up had smudged, and her eyes were mascara blackened and puffy.

"There you go." Jess said angrily. "Are you happy now?"

"What happened, love?"

"Take a wild guess. Tom James." Jess sobbed.

"Did he try it on?"

"Almost. He made suggestions."

"What happened?"

"Don't make me tell you."

"I'm guessing you didn't get a deal then."

"Oh, no. I scored a six record deal, with a million pound advance. Of course I didn't get a bloody deal."

"There's no need to be like that." May protested.

"I disagree. Actually, I think there's every need. You knew exactly what that… what that beast was like, and you made me go in there, more or less dressed up as bait, just so he'd try his luck. Did you reckon he might just want to make my dreams come true so he could lust after me some more? Or did you think I might actually go through with it?"

"Babe, I never meant…"

Jess interrupted May. "That's it though. You never do mean it. You never think, do you, Mags? I made the mistake of trying to do this your way. And oh yes, let us look what happened? Absolutely nothing. Well, nothing to be of any use to me. What about my way? What about me?"

"I'm sorry, Jess. I'm so fucking sorry. I made a call, and I got it wrong. I wish I could help you properly. I tell you what. Next time, we'll try a different approach. How about that?" May smiled hopefully.

"There won't be a next time. I'm giving up this stupid game. It isn't my world. Oh, and to top it off, not only is he a total letch, but he's a complete imbecile too. If that is what this business is like, then perhaps I'm better off not having to deal with idiots like him."

May's demeanour changed. She stood up, stepping away from Jess without turning away.

"That's it. Walk away. Turn your back on it. Waste all those years of practice, hide from who you are and what you can do if you want, but you know that it'll always be there. You'll always ask yourself what you missed out on. Jess, I don't know how to convince you. You are a proper talent. A real star. There's more than one way to use your ability." May looked to the ceiling. "Okay. I made a massive mistake, but I know that there is a place for you in this music business. Don't let that little wanker destroy you. If you do that, then he's got away with it completely."

Jess sighed. She tried her best to wipe away the smudges of make-up. The quiver of sadness filled her lungs.

"For the first time in ages, I think we might actually agree."

May smiled warmly "I'm so happy to hear you say that. The thought of you giving up just scares me. You are way too good to jack it in."

"So you keep saying. I still don't really believe you." Jess said.

"Trust me. It really is no more than a matter of time."

Jess and May hugged. Eventually, Jess edged away and looked at May.

"You were wrong about him getting away with it completely though."

"Why? Did you call the police?"

"I wanted to, but I thought it might have been a bit tricky after I broke his nose."

May laughed. "You did what?"

"I punched him and broke his nose. I've never hit anybody before. I doubt I ever will again, but it felt good."

"Fair enough. I must remember never to really piss you off though."

Jess put up a guard. "I'm warning you!"

May instinctively grabbed Jessica's hands and kissed her swollen knuckle. "I really am so sorry."

Jessica's phone danced around maniacally on her dressing table. The caller ID gave no clues, other than it being a Central London number.

"Hello?" Jess said, worried that it might be related to the Impact incident.

"Oh, hello. Is that Miss Jessica Vaughan?" A warm but authoritative voice asked.

"Yes. It is. Can I ask who's calling?"

"Sorry, my name is Alison Harrison. I work for Bold, Harrison and Stronge Solicitors. We are acting as the executors for the estate of the late Miss Margaret O'Sullivan. Firstly, let me express my deepest sympathies."

"Thank you. Sometimes it is difficult to believe that she's not still here."

Jess looked across at May, who was lighting another cigarette to go with the tequila that she was now drinking. She pulled an exaggerated grin. May responded by blowing a giant kiss.

"Secondly, were you aware that Miss O'Sullivan had a will?"

"No? We never discussed it."

"Don't worry, people seldom do. I can tell you now, that you are one of the named beneficiaries. Would it be possible for you to make an appointment to come into our office?"

"Sure. When would be suitable?"

"Well, Miss Vaughan, the other beneficiaries are coming in tomorrow afternoon. You'd be welcome to join them. Would you like me to text you the address?"

"Yes, please. That would be perfect. What time would you like me?"

"Lovely. The others are coming in for 1pm. I'll look forward to seeing you then. And I am truly sorry for your loss."

"Thank you. Good bye." Jess hung up her phone and turned to May. "What have you left me?"

May tapped the side of her nose. "You'll see, darling, you'll see."

Chapter 24

Within seconds of finishing, Jess had left Mickey and May and rushed into the garden. She spun around on the patio. The warm summer evening was yielding to a sticky summer night, but small garden lanterns were doing their best to offer some illumination. It wasn't much, but it fought off the worst of the growing darkness. Her eyes followed the path into the darkness by the small pond at the bottom of the garden. It was then that she saw Nick. He appeared to be skulking behind a large established tree.

"I promise you. Nobody knows anything. Of course I'm not going to say. I can't come now, I won't be able to get away. I'm at a party with Jess. That's going to look even more suspicious, don't you think?" Nick whispered.

"Who are you talking to, Nick?"

"Jess. I didn't see you." Nick smiled awkwardly.

"The phone?"

"What?"

"Who are you talking to, Nick?"

"It's only work. There's a problem with an order." He replied abruptly.

"Where did you go?"

"What?"

"When I got up to sing."

"Jess, you know I can't watch you sing."

"It wasn't just me, was it?" Jess was starting to get defensive.

"Oh, and that makes it better? You're an embarrassment."

"I beg your pardon?"

"You and them. Like an east end knees-up in some shitty boozer."

"Fine. If you feel like that, I suppose it's best if you go outside then." Jess seethed.

"I'm sorry, babe. I don't want to hurt you, I just find watching you so awkward."

"Have you got to go in then?" She asked, knowing what he would say.

"What?"

"Work. You said there was a problem."

"Do you mind?"

"You go. I'll be fine here."

Nick stepped forward to kiss Jess on the cheek. Jess backed away.

"I'll go and say goodbye to Mags. Hopefully, I'll be home before breakfast."

"Go on then, you sort them out."

Jess stood in the garden, alone. She looked up at the darkening sky. There was barely a star to be seen. The darkness of the evening conveniently concealed the tear that was running down her cheek.

"Is everything okay, Jessica?" Jake had appeared again, more or less from nowhere.

"Hi Jake. Yeah, I'm fine."

"Here, I've got you a drink."

"Thanks."

Jake passed a champagne flute over to Jess. She looked at him and smiled.

"Have you been crying?" Jake asked.

"It's nothing." Jess lied. "Did you want me for something?"

"Not really." Jake lied. "I just wanted to say how good you were in the kitchen."

"Thanks. I enjoyed it. Usually, I'm not keen on playing live."

"That's a shame. What a total waste. Lovely choice of song, too. Not an obvious choice either."

"David Bowie was one of my heroes. I've loved him since I was a toddler."

"I met him once. Lovely guy. He was everything you'd hope for. A bit crackers, but so friendly and down to earth."

"Okay. Now I'm jealous."

Jess and Jake laughed together. Briefly, their eyes met. For a fraction of a second, Jess imagined kissing him before her morals checked her.

"Hey, I'm trying to get into a bit of music production. Would you fancy getting involved with that? Nothing too heavy."

"Between work and Nick, I don't really have much free time. Sounds interesting, though."

"I hope so. It's more for fun than anything else. I couldn't give it up completely."

"I didn't realise that you were still playing."

"I do a bit now and then. I prefer the studio though, nobody hears your mistakes that way."

"Are you not going to get up and play a song or two?" Jess asked.

"Me? I think Mags would probably throw me in the pond if I did that."

"She loves you. You know that."

"Yeah. I know. It's mutual. She's a special soul." Jake looked around the garden, nervously. "Now, I know this is a grinding change of gear, but would you like to play one of my live music nights?"

"Oh God. Erm… I don't…"

"I'll understand if you don't want to."

"No, I do. It's just that…"

"Stage fright?"

"Sort of." Jess lied for convenience. "I don't play live very often anymore."

"You should. You really should." Jake's eyes twinkled as he smiled. "Can I have your telephone number?"

"I'm sorry?" Jess asked, taken aback.

"I'll give you mine."

"I can't. I mean…"

"When you do want a gig, you can call me, and I'll know who it is."

"Oh." Jess didn't know whether to be relieved or disappointed.

"You didn't think I was…"

"No. Goodness, no."

"I know you've got a boyfriend. I wouldn't want you to think I was making a pass."

"That's fine. I understand. Here, pass me your mobile."

Jess took Jake's phone and rang her own.

"I'm going to go now before I embarrass myself anymore."

Jake slowly edged away, embarrassed and scared that he had said the wrong thing.

"That's fine. I'm okay."

"Will you call me then?"

"We'll see." Jess smiled cheekily.

Chapter 25

Jess walked along the landing of her block of flats. There was a wide smile on her face and a bouncing spring to her step. The spring sun felt warm on her face as she reached her front door. She slid her key into the lock, and opened it up, full of delight.

"May Mornington, you are one crafty cow. Thank you so much. How on earth can I ever repay you?" Jess shouted as she closed her front door behind her.

Instantly, she felt alone.

"May? Mags? Are you there? Stop messing about."

Jess looked around her immaculately tidied flat. Suddenly, it seemed so big, so empty.

"It's not funny. Just come out. Please?"

Jess carried out a thorough search of her flat. There seemed to be no evidence at all that May had ever been there. Everywhere was clean, tidy and neat. She slumped onto the freshly plumped sofa. It was then that she saw it in front of her. On the coffee table was a notepad, a virtually empty bottle of whiskey with a glass, and a cigarette with a box of matches. As Jess moved the objects one by one, she could see a note, handwritten on the pad. With trembling hands, she reached out and picked it up.

"Hey Chick,

I guess you've worked out that I'm gone now. I'd like to think that the last few weeks have saved us both. It's time for the two of us to move on though.

I'm not very good at goodbyes. I wish it didn't have to end like this, but I needed to go. You might have told me I could stay forever, but I fear that if I hadn't left now, then I never would have.

Call Jake. He might be going through a mid-life crisis, but he really is a good bloke. But before you do that, have a drink and a smoke on me.

All my love always,

Mags

x

P.S. You really are fucking awesome."

Jess poured the whiskey, lit the cigarette and cried like a baby.

Chapter 26

This is the last will and testament of Margaret Aisling Geraldine O'Sullivan. Well, actually, it isn't. I read the first draft, and it made no sense to me, and I wrote that one with the solicitor. This is a letter, in plain English, that lets you know what I want to happen. So, Annie, Jess, Jake and Tyler, this is really for you. I'll leave the technical stuff to the professionals.

Seeing as this letter is being read out by a very posh and very expensive solicitor, I'd like to say 'big hairy fanny'. Legally, if they want their money, they have to read that.

I always had a feeling that it would end like this. I never wanted to hurt you, but I couldn't go on with how my life had become.

Annie, you have been the best agent and manager that I could imagine. Take £50,000.

Tyler, you've been a pain in the arse since we were 18. I love you for it. Take £50,000.

Jake, I'm giving you my guitars. Some of them are actually older than you are. Sell them if you want, but please keep the Rickenbacker. It's beautiful. Thank you for everything.

Jess. My love, my soulmate. I'm giving you £30,000 every year, but it comes with a couple of conditions:

1. You must record and release an album at least every five years. This must always be available for sale.

2. You must play to a paying audience no less than six times a year.

If you don't manage both of these conditions, then you're not getting a penny.

You should join forces with Jake. He may be a mid-life crisis in expensive jeans, but if I could make music with a little weirdo with criminal halitosis like Mickey George, then you can put up with an old has-been like him.

I have asked my solicitor to set up a trust to fund scholarships for young musicians from poor backgrounds to go to LSMP. Hopefully, this can run for many years.

Please liquidate my remaining assets and pass everything that may be left on to prostate cancer charities. It may have killed my darling Mickey, but perhaps I can stop it happening to other people.

Please donate all my future royalties to women's charities in London. Life can be shit for a poor girl on her own.

All my love always,

MMxx

Chapter 27

"Hello?"

"Hi, is that Jake?" Jess asked.

"Jess? Are you alright?" Jake replied with concern.

"I think so. I know it's only been a couple of weeks since the will reading, but I don't suppose you would like to help me with recording and releasing some music?"

"I'd love to. I can't think of anything I'd prefer to do."

"Great. Would you like to go out for a drink as well?" Jess asked hesitantly.

"What, to discuss the music?"

"Not really. Just a drink or two. I think I'd just like to get to know you." Jess smiled to herself.

"That'd be great."

Printed in Great Britain
by Amazon